EYE
OF THE
HURRICANE 1

Dean Landers

This is a work of fiction. Names, characters, places, and incidents are products of the author's imagination or are used fictitiously and are not to be construed as real. Any resemblance to actual events, locations, organizations, or persons, living or dead, is entirely coincidental.

World Castle Publishing, LLC
Pensacola, Florida

Copyright © Dean Landers 2017
Paperback ISBN: 9781629897332
eBook ISBN: 9781629897349
First Edition World Castle Publishing, LLC, July 17, 2017
http://www.worldcastlepublishing.com

Licensing Notes

Cover: Karen Fuller
Editor: Lisa Petrocelli

Dedicated to:
Mum and Dad

For purchasing my first typewriter and
clipping out my newspaper articles

Table of Contents

CHAPTER ONE
INTO THE FRAY

The deepening swell rushes over the vessel, causing a severe rolling motion that slams me against a wall in the command center. For the last several hours, as the waves and winds got higher and higher and the storm rolled back and forth over us, I had been hanging out in the head purging my heaving guts in spasms of sickness.

What did I get myself into here? I asked myself, reflecting upon the course of events that led to this moment. I know this uniquely designed vessel is engineered to be virtually indestructible in the worst seas the world's oceans can throw at it. However, a worm of doubt is crawling into my frayed consciousness, betraying the unwavering confidence I once had in this insane project.

A lifelong confirmed news junkie, I habitually monitored CNN and various news feeds available on my computer and phone, searching for the worst disasters and biggest calamities occurring all over the planet. A deep curiosity about world events fed this news craving, also fueled by another compunction that I was less proud of and wrestled with constantly.

The truth was that my fascination with the news pushed into the background my concern for personal issues and problems I was confronting in my own life. People in the news were always worse off than I was, so I could beat my chest with the positive feeling that my life wasn't so bad. Others had darker destinies than my own.

Actually, many psychologists assert that the process of putting your life in healthy perspective in the context of larger society, serves to achieve a level of self-awareness and greater peace of mind that is highly desirable.

Excessive self-absorption to the exclusion of awareness of matters beyond self has been the downfall of many. Fortunately, I hold that enlightened self-awareness rests upon the notion *we are all in this together*, that the achievement of mutually positive outcomes is the holy grail of human civilization.

But how did I make this transition from a typical news fanatic to being in the middle of a one-of-a-kind news event. This turn of events was remarkable and unexpected.

Wall-to-wall media coverage of Hurricane Katrina beamed from all channels and news media, describing an unprecedented storm developing in the Caribbean, preparing to smash into the Gulf Coast at some point in the next few days. Katrina had already hit Cuba and other Caribbean islands causing millions of dollars of damage and taking many lives. Weather satellites and related instruments were locked into collection of real-time storm data that was constantly being fed into supercomputers and spewed out as updated storm projections of path, power and intensity.

Predicting hurricanes had come a long way since hurricanes and other extreme weather events were viewed as God's displeasure with the world. Due to speedy movement of extreme weather phenomena, slow communications systems in the early days prevented people from receiving advance news of bad weather.

Horses and ships didn't travel faster than weather patterns moving across the planet. The invention of the telegraph in the nineteenth century enabled weather information to be wired to communities in the path of storms. Fast forward to the early twenty-first century and weather analysis and prediction technologies were leapfrogging themselves every few years.

Satellites beamed weather data down to supercomputers, enabling satellite feeds to be interpolated with ground information gathered by radar, weather stations, and other related technologies. The resulting weather models were achieving higher and higher accuracy rates, providing people timely advance notice of weather events affecting their area.

However, due to the increase of global-warming-related extreme weather events, including hurricanes, droughts, wildfires, and superstorms, there were some noticeable gaps in the capabilities of technologies used to gather weather data.

One deficiency in hurricane prediction was the lack of real-time data on surface conditions in hurricane waters. Hurricane hunter aircraft were able to fly into hurricanes and gather weather data from onboard instruments and sensors dropped from these planes. Also, weather sensor buoys were placed on the ocean in the vicinity of hurricanes and allowed to drift through the storm, gathering data and transmitting it to shore stations, planes, or satellites.

However, were these existing technologies enough to monitor hurricanes and gather useful data about these disastrous weather events?

CHAPTER TWO
REALITY

Survivorman and *Dual Survival* are probably my favorite reality shows. Les Stroud, a Canadian, loves being out in the bush and coming up with strategies and tools to stay alive in desperate survival situations. Les has no camera crew with him and does all his own photography while negotiating the perils of the particular survival situation he is replicating on each *Survivorman* episode. Stroud has a safety crew located a few miles away in case he runs into real trouble and cannot bail himself out. To his credit, Stroud rarely needs the safety crew to come in and save him.

Dual Survival, hosted by Americans, Cody Lundin and Joseph Teti, is premised upon the idea of two people working as a team to extricate themselves from various survival scenarios. *Dual Survival* is entertaining and educational, providing specific techniques and information to laypersons who may stray off the beaten path and need to secure their

11

own rescue.

Reality shows in all of their manifestations, from *Survivorman* to *Axe Men* to *Deadliest Catch*, all push the envelope of human endurance and stress tolerance for the entertainment and enlightenment of the vast untested masses sprawled in front of their flat screens on La-Z-Boys or couches. In my view, most people tend to choose the path of least resistance in their life choices, "safe" and "sure" being the mantra of their caution-based lifestyles.

Unfortunately, if all humanity opted for the caution-based approach to life, we would still be living in caves and foraging off the land. There have always been people who defied the status quo and ventured into uncharted waters—like inventing the spear, cultivating crops, introducing the wheel, developing electrical systems and devices, to name but a few.

Without risk there is no reward, or conversely, no reward without risk. Fortune favors the bold and fails the meek. Thoughts must be translated into action in order for progress to be achieved.

Over the years, I had come up with numerous ideas for reality shows. After all, reality is limitless in all its manifestations and possibilities. But I didn't want to be involved in a staged reality show with no real purpose or value other than entertainment. I wanted to do something that had never been done, to go where no man or woman had ever been before.

While I was watching news coverage of Hurricane Katrina, the wheels started clicking over in my mind and a unique idea began to take shape. There is something missing in this picture, I thought. Many wise people have said that if you really want to understand something, you need to place yourself right in the thick of it. An aspiring football player must get out on the field and get knocked around a bit, before he really starts to understand the game. A would-be politician must actually run for office, even if only for dogcatcher to start, to get a real handle on the electoral process.

Or, as Teddy Roosevelt more aptly put it: "It is not the critic who counts; not the man who points out how the strong man stumbles, or where the doer of deeds could have done them better. The credit belongs to the man who is actually in the arena, whose face is marred by dust and sweat and blood; who strives valiantly; who errs, who comes short again and again, because there is no effort without error and shortcoming; but who does actually strive to do the deeds; who knows great enthusiasms, the great devotions; who spends himself in a worthy cause; who at the best knows in the end the triumph of high achievement, and who at the worst, if he fails, at least fails while daring greatly, so that his place shall never be with those cold and timid souls who neither know victory nor defeat."

CHAPTER THREE
DEEP BLUE

I have always been fascinated by the sea and sailing, imagining myself roaming the oceans with Captain Cook or Joshua Slocum, the first person to sail around the world single-handed in 1896, on his little self-built boat, *The Spray*. Slocum was a mariner of the first order, having earned his stripes as a blue water sailor on the merchant sailing ships of the mid-nineteenth century.

Only a boy when he first went to sea, Slocum acquired his sailing skills and knowledge the real way, by mastering the multifold aspects of navigating a ship by wind power alone. When steam-powered ships became the norm in the late nineteenth century, Slocum was a man whose time had passed, who was cast adrift in the modern machine-based industrial world.

From the days of Slocum acrobatically maneuvering around the pitching rigging and storm-

15

tossed decks of a three-masted merchant schooner, maritime technology advanced exponentially through the twentieth century, turning the corner into the twenty-first century with a bigger splash, as giant container ships with massive cargoes plied the world's waterways with clockwork precision. Manned by skeleton crews, these blue water behemoths were guided largely by computers, with the human component of the ship's operation consigned to monitoring the computers and checking the load.

The voyage of the first United States nuclear powered submarine, *The Nautilus,* under the polar ice cap in 1958, heralded a new age in undersea warfare and exploration. This new generation of atomic age submarines could stay underwater for extended periods and launch multiple nuclear intercontinental ballistic missiles at the drop of a hat. Nuclear submarines roaming the world's oceans became the cornerstone of nuclear deterrence, the key to MAD-Mutually Assured Destruction. Even if the United States was obliterated by nuclear missiles, this deadly submarine fleet could invoke massive retaliation and retribution, tearing the enemy to shreds.

If all the above was possible, I concluded, why couldn't we design and build a new type of nuclear-powered ocean research vessel that could go anywhere at any time, handling the worst conditions the world's oceans could throw at it, while gathering on-the-spot weather data that could save thousands of lives and billions of dollars in property damage.

CHAPTER FOUR
CRACKPOT

When you advocate something that has never been done before, you are often labeled a "crackpot," drawing fire from all and sundry individuals who think you are absolutely crazy. "If it hasn't been done before there is a reason for that, it is a dumb idea," some people will say; or "That idea is too far out there," "That guy is a nut," or, most commonly the thought that is rarely voiced, "I'm jealous because I didn't think of it."

People in business and government present themselves as supporting innovation in all its forms, but when push comes to shove are they really behind new ways of approaching problems? The Germans set the world standard for high quality road construction, building the famous Autobahn highway in the 1930s involving the best engineers, newest technology, and with a concerted effort and a burning desire to build the longest lasting, smoothest road possible.

The United States did the same with the Apollo Space Program in the 1960s, assembling a team of the best and brightest and putting a man on the moon in July 1969. However, the Autobahn and the Apollo Space Program are exceptions that prove the rule. The United States infrastructure is crumbling due to blatant inattention and mismanagement, with short-term budget-to-budget thinking combined with a negligent lack of foresight and ignoring the old saying, "An ounce of prevention is worth a pound of cure." Build a road or bridge properly in the first place, then maintain it regularly so you don't have to rebuild it from scratch when it crumbles. Billions of dollars would be saved in this way, and a reliable, well-maintained infrastructure would boost the economy and keep us competitive with China and other emerging global powers.

Another dent in the armor of innovation are those that have vested interests in the status quo. Their rice bowl is filled by doing things the old way so they see no need to change. Of course, convincing these old-school individuals they would be better off adopting new technologies and methods is like trying to force a chicken to lay golf balls rather than eggs. Everybody gets older and more conservative and cautious, but that doesn't mean they need to close off their minds completely. Mother Nature teaches that to survive you must adapt to constantly changing circumstances and conditions. To stick your head in the sand is to sign your own death warrant.

After several weeks of calling everyone I could think of, from governments to corporations to venture capitalists and getting a totally negative response, I began to get disillusioned about my idea. Maybe my plan of building and deploying a new type of ocean research ship that could gather real-time, ground zero data about hurricanes and other extreme weather events, is a no-go proposition. Maybe I should hang it up and join a senior's ping-pong club to vent my frustrations.

Everyone in my personal circle, knowing I'm always working on some crazy, impossible scheme or new business idea, paid lip service to my constant ramblings about the new research vessel I wanted to build. The idea would lie dormant within me for weeks or months, then I would suddenly get a lightning bolt of inspiration to advance the project forward. This burst of energy would continue for a few days until I ran into another roadblock and the cycle would repeat itself.

My wife, Honeybunch, a huge Facebook fan, told me to put the idea on Facebook and see what happened. Perhaps with everyone networking, someone would come forward out of the digital mist to help get the project off the ground and into the water. I kept posting the idea in different ways on Facebook, hoping to wake some angel out of their slumber. I got plenty of replies but it was the usual innocuous Facebook chatter — people whining about different things or describing day to day personal life minutiae, as if they were the first humans to drive a car, go shopping, meet a friend for lunch, or get hammered at a party. Boring, boring, boring.

One day I groggily awoke late in the morning from a long deep sleep, the kind of sleep I usually had, and turned on my cell phone. I checked my e-mail, phone, and text messages then went on Facebook to see what was cooking there. My eccentric cousin Andy had sent me another slew of messages about the history of rock and roll with photos of every band to have played since Elvis, "The King of Rock and Roll," lit up the music scene in the early 1950s. At the end of Andy's rant was the weirdest posting he had ever sent me.

There was no music photo in the post nor any graphics or color of any kind. In fact, the posting only had one five-letter word in large black lettering: CROWD. What did this mean? What was Andy trying to tell me with the word "crowd"? Andy knew that I didn't generally like crowds, preferring my own company or a small coterie of friends or family.

So I sent a message to Andy asking what he meant by his crowd post. Andy replied promptly, stating that he really didn't know what he meant by crowd, he was drunk at the time in a busy bar. But, upon further reflection, Andy realized that crowd had nothing to do with crowds at bars as he drank in taverns regularly and liked socializing with wall-to-wall intoxicated bodies. He finally said, "You will have to figure it out for yourself."

I was perplexed with this conundrum for several weeks, waking up in cold sweats in the middle of the night trying to figure out what this crowd post was all about. At the same time, I was still at a loss as to how I would get my research vessel project going.

One morning I was going through Google News posts in the business section and noticed a write-up about crowd-funding, a method of obtaining capital for producing movies, starting businesses, raising money for nonprofit organizations, and a variety of other purposes. Given that banks were loaning less and less money to individuals and small businesses, and venture capital was very difficult to obtain, more and more people were turning to crowd-funding to convert their dreams into reality.

CHAPTER FIVE
NUTS AND BOLTS

I had already investigated possible designs for my vessel and contacted government agencies, private organizations, and nonprofits involved in weather research, including deployment of specialized data-gathering vessels. I even contacted a retired naval architect who was willing to collaborate with me to design a new research vessel that I decided to name *Eye 1*, or in longer form, *Eye of the Hurricane 1*. We looked at a number of different ship and submarine designs and probed the latest cutting-edge technologies developed for these vessels.

At the same time I studied the history of hurricanes and examined the elements of wind, water, ocean temperature, global weather patterns, and other variables comprising a full-blown hurricane or super typhoon. These weather events are two sides of the same coin, called different names depending on what part of the world you were in.

23

After consultation with other experts, I determined that a boat or submarine with conventional speed capabilities wasn't going to cut the mustard in terms of being able to catch up to and follow hurricanes. The fastest research ships travel 30+ miles per hour and nuclear submarines, although their exact top speeds are classified, can travel in the 40 mph range under water. These speeds, although fast, weren't even close to what was needed to catch up to a rapidly developing hurricane and stay in the middle of it.

I seemed to be at a dead end with no way to achieve the vessel performance capabilities my over-the-top project required.

Then one day I was talking with my naval architect advisor and the subject of the popular movie, *The Hunt for Red October*, came up. In the 1991 movie, starring Sean Connery and Alec Baldwin, a new generation Russian nuclear submarine not yet known by Western intelligence, is sent on a clandestine mission across the Atlantic Ocean to New York, to test a totally new, super quiet propulsion technology. If it worked as designed, this new supercavitation stealth propulsion system could not be detected by any state-of-the-art submarine hunter technology, thus upsetting the delicate MAD-Mutually Assured Destruction-balance of power between the Soviet Bloc and the United States and its allies.

Armed with powerful nuclear missiles, these new

Red October class nuclear submarines could lie close to the United States coastline and quickly destroy major American cities and military targets before we had a chance to respond in kind. Also, undetectable by the United States Navy, Soviet Red October class subs could easily shadow and destroy United States naval vessels, including our nuclear subs.

My response to the architect, who I code-named Arch, was quick and unrestrained: "What has a fictional submarine in a fictional movie got to do with our Eye 1 project?" Arch didn't bat an eye and responded, "The supercavitation technology is real and has been worked on by both the Russians and us for quite some time. In fact, the United States Navy is currently in the advanced research and development phase of a new supercavitation-propelled submarine called the *Underwater Express*. Information regarding the current status of this new vessel has not been released."

The Russians are the only nation with experimental supercavitation torpedoes called Shkval with rocket engines that enable these torpedoes to cruise toward their targets at speeds in excess of 200 mph. Also, the Japanese have developed new ships that utilize supercavitation technology that cuts fuel consumption by 25 percent by blowing air bubbles under the ship's hull to reduce friction."

Cavitation technology is the process wherein

an object moves so fast through water that it creates a gas bubble around itself so that most of the hull is in direct contact with the gas bubble and not the water. Unencumbered by the high drag of water, the object is free to speed along at much higher speeds than are otherwise possible. The top speed of a small supercavitation vessel is predicted at 127 mph.

Thus, the completed and fully operational Eye 1 supercavitation vessel could sit in the vicinity where most hurricanes form, then launch at top speed to intercept the eye of the hurricane. Most hurricanes that hit the United States begin either in the Caribbean or the Atlantic. Many of the worst hurricanes start off the coast of Africa. Like all tropical cyclones, a hurricane needs the warm water of the tropics, which feeds a storm with energy, in order to form. The atmosphere must be laden with moisture.

Now that I found the right technology to get my Eye 1 project going, I needed to implement my crowd-funding idea to raise money to build this unique new vessel. Also, I must find volunteers to man Eye 1 on her groundbreaking research missions. Who would want to risk their lives barreling along at 127 mph under water so they can gather scientific data in the middle of the eye of a hurricane?

CHAPTER SIX
MONEY, MONEY, MONEY

It was a beautiful spring day and I was sitting out in my front yard enjoying the sunshine with my best friend Osho, a five-year-old chow-lab mix that was abandoned by its previous owner and wound up at the local humane society. It was love at first sight for my family when we were introduced to Osho, a small seventeen pound bundle of energy, in the fenced-in pen adjacent the local humane society building. Osho was home with us the next day.

I carefully consumed a cold beverage, also known as a barley sandwich in Canada, while Osho watched the cars passing in front of our house and smelled the scents coming from the greenbelt area nearby.

I picked up my cell phone and called Arch, my naval architect advisor, to get the cost estimates for building Eye 1. I knew that designing and building this new high-tech vessel was going to be very expensive, but I did not know how pricey it would be.

"Plug," Arch said, "it is not looking good at all. My estimate of the cost of designing and constructing Eye 1 is in the $175,000,000 to $200,000,000 category. I don't know where or how we can get this type of money." I responded with, "I don't know either, Arch, a few bake sales and potluck dinners won't get the job done. I am in the process of putting a post on a crowd-funding site to see how much we can raise there."

CHAPTER SEVEN
GURU

Backed up against all four walls, I knew there was only one answer to my dilemma — to go and see my guru for advice. Unfortunately my guru did not live down the street in a three-bedroom ranch. He lived in a self-built cabin far past the end of the road in the wilderness of British Columbia, Canada, so far off the grid that only a handful of his closest friends knew where to find him.

In my old Ford Ranger four-wheel-drive truck, I carefully negotiated the ancient rutted logging path, once a well-maintained road that had supported many large logging trucks transporting logs to local sawmills in the 1950s. Due to the high cost of maintaining logging roads, only currently used logging roads are kept in good shape, then allowed to go fallow after the wood is harvested.

The scenery was spectacular: snow-capped peaks contrasting with thick green forests blanketing the mountainsides and valley bottoms. I grew up with these resplendent mountain vistas and never tired of their majesty. I eased my truck up a steep incline in four-wheel-drive low, trying to avoid boulders and other debris covering this sketchy trail. Once on the crest of the ridge, I looked down a precipitous slope dropping to a deep canyon with a foaming river at its base. Slowly, I made my way down the winding road to a ledge jutting over the steep drop to the water.

I checked my GPS and map with instructions Hatch had sent me by snail mail a couple of months before. I got out of my truck, threw on my heavy backpack, and assessed the narrow trail carved out of the cliff by local Indians several hundred years before. The Indians had worked with the natural curves and indentations of the rocky canyon wall to create a path that was barely negotiable by thin people on clear rain-free days, much less rotund individuals who struggled to get through doors or ease their way into automobiles. Needless to say, these early natives got plenty of exercise in their hunting and gathering lifestyle, with not an extra ounce on their lithe frames.

Luckily my slim body was able to inch its way down the terrifying route to the river with only my backpack occasionally bumping the rock face on the uphill side of the trail. At the flat rock outcrop at the bottom, I set my pack down and examined the class six rapids surging down the canyon. The rapids enveloped boulders with thick foam and giant back waves that caused my spine to tingle with the possibility of overturning in the water and smashing against one of these refrigerator-sized obstacles.

Then I ate some whole grain bars, filled my canteen with river water, and popped a water purification pill into the container, drinking the water after it was purified twenty minutes later. I was excited at the possibility of seeing Hatch again after several years. Hatch Moniker, also known as Mad Dog to his forestry colleagues, was a one of a kind eccentric with a heart of gold and a love of nature exceeded by no one I ever met.

Mad Dog Moniker also had a wild streak that made him famous in the forest service for jumping creeks with a snowmobile and going over a cliff in a snowmobile, saved by the soft snow at the bottom that absorbed the impact of his snow machine crashing down the ninety-foot incline. And he was the fastest in a forestry truck, always tearing along iffy forest access roads at breakneck speeds that defied all physics of back road travel, as if his truck was glued to the dirt path.

When I was first assigned to the remote forestry post where Hatch worked, I was nervous about this new work situation, worrying that people wouldn't like me or I wouldn't fit in. When I showed up at the forestry station for my first day of work, Hatch immediately invited me down in the basement to see his office. I stepped into his office and he closed the door behind us where a surprise awaited me inside the door. Solidly affixed to the inside of Hatch's government office door was a dartboard.

As I stood amazed that Hatch would have the chutzpah to defy forest service regulations by putting a dartboard on his door, Hatch handed me some darts and we started playing. I asked Hatch the obvious question: "What happens if someone comes in the door while you are throwing darts?" Hatch replied, "Tough luck." After a few rounds of darts and kibitzing with Hatch, I began to relax and think that this was a place I could enjoy. My nature and strict rules and conformist behavior, mixed like oil and water. Hatch was a kindred spirit.

I quickly rolled out my small rubber raft which inflated automatically, then assembled my paddles, which had been separated into two pieces each to fit in my pack. I looked at the turbulent water with great trepidation, imagining myself flipping over into the cold water on the first set of rapids, then thrashing around in the water until I pulled myself up on the shoreline, wet, soggy, and chilled to the bone.

I remembered a wedding back in the early 1980s when a bunch of us got drunk and climbed into a rubber raft before flipping over in the first set of rapids of a well-known *Deliverance*-type canyon, our timing and coordination nonexistent in the stupefied state we were in. Many canoes, kayaks, rafts, and several lives had been claimed by this section of river over the years. We barely made it out of the water and hiked back to our vehicles, significantly worse for wear after being pummeled and tossed by the raging river waters.

But since then I had improved my skills as a river rat, learning the finer points of staying afloat when that didn't seem to be possible. My older brother Radisson had been mentored by local whitewater expert Etienne Brule and passed this knowledge along to me, causing my confidence to rise and my abilities to soar.

I carefully stowed my pack in a large dry bag which I tied into the front section of the raft, then cast off quickly, paddling hard toward the middle of the river so I didn't get slammed into the sheer cliff face downriver from my launching point. Once in the main channel I was able to maneuver around a big boulder before hurtling into a larger set of rapids, making me dance around this set of hazards with my paddles dug in deep with hard steady strokes.

This struggle continued for fifteen minutes until I shot out the end of the vortex into calmer waters, breathing a heavy sigh of relief as I laid back in the raft for a brief respite from the intense action.

Several more sets of rapids followed before the

river widened and the land opened up on each side of the watercourse. Now I was looking for a special marker that Hatch indicated on his map as the place I was to go ashore and start hiking to his cabin. A few minutes later I spotted an Indian pictograph on a large rock on the right side of the river. The drawing depicted a grizzly bear with several arrows in its side, etched on the rock with charcoal and ground-down plants in liquid form, faded, but standing the test of time quite well.

I pulled up onshore and grabbed my pack out of the dry bag before stuffing my raft and dry bag under a dense thicket of bushes so that no one would find them. Hatch was insistent I left no clues that would reveal to anyone this location had any special significance.

The next part of my journey was a grinding thirty-mile hike to Hatch's cabin hidden away on a small high altitude lake several watersheds over. The altitude changes and scarcity of trails would require at least three days of hard travel in this wilderness country.

The quiet of the forest calmed my nerves and caused me to reach back into my memory banks to a period when I spent most of my time in these forests. I had been a wilderness recreation mapper for the forest service in the late 70s and early 80s, a position that required extensive travel in trucks, airplanes, snowmobiles, skis, canoes, and many days on foot.

The goal of this fieldwork was to determine the potential of crown forest lands for various outdoor recreation activities including fishing, hunting, camping, skiing, hiking, boating, canoeing, and countless other forest recreation pursuits. High quality recreation areas would be carefully noted so that logging and other resource extraction activities would dovetail with recreation in the best way possible within the multiple use forestry management framework.

Tourism was a big revenue generator in these parts, providing many jobs in the forest industry and other natural resource-based sectors. Canadians were historically known as "hewers of wood and drawers of water," given their heavy reliance on natural resources.

I gradually humped up a steep pitch through thick Devil's Club, a prickly plant that grows abundantly in low altitude, well-watered areas and is the nemesis of many a hiker and backpacker, stopping them in their tracks. Fortunately, I had thick clothing and heavy boots on, the sharp barbs making minimal entry through my outerwear to prick my skin.

My goal for the first day was to reach a small creek about ten miles away and camp there. Water is an important consideration in any backpacking trip where sweat comes in waves due to the heavy exertion required to move a fifty-pound pack across the mottled, up and down landscape. Over the years I had developed a steady measured hiking pace that gobbled up the trail at a consistent rate with few rest breaks, unlike the jerky stops and starts of a novice burning himself out before any real distance gains were achieved.

Hatch was always in superb physical shape, lifting weights five or six hours a day and running around town to complete his errands. His passion for physical fitness and brute strength derived from his low self-esteem as a boy, when he viewed himself as a ninety-eight-pound weakling. Hatch's other interest was reading books from his vast library containing many volumes on philosophy, nature, poetry, and a variety of other subjects. He valued books as the repository of wisdom and knowledge, reprimanding any miscreant borrower that curled a page or bent a cover or otherwise tarnished his printed treasures.

Also, Hatch was a lot of fun to be around. Often at lunch, Hatch and I and a new minted professional forester named Woody, fresh out of forestry school in Alberta and getting his fiery baptism in managing the thick woodland areas our ranger district was comprised of, would head down to a strip joint for lunch. A few beers and a burger later, we enjoyed the eye candy in front of us, cheering and hurrahing the dancers performing particularly sexy moves for our pleasure. And, after a day working in the bush, hot, dusty, and horny as we were, Hatch always drove through the middle of town, on a street he called "Pussy Lane," as we scanned the sidewalks for hot babes emerging from offices or stores.

In his second marriage, trouble had been brewing between Hatch and his wife Shirley for quite some time, the exact cause of the disharmony not readily discernible to Hatch's friends. They knew he deeply missed his daughters living with their mother two thousand miles away in Ontario, but surmised this wasn't the whole story of the marriage meltdown.

In fear of the cold war turning hot, Hatch was heavily influenced by the Vietnam War, where he served as a Navy Seal in the late 1960s. Hatch rarely mentioned his combat experiences, but talked about the regular nightmares he experienced due to the bloody gruesomeness of the protracted war. A gentle person to his core, Hatch had trouble reconciling his quiet nature with the dispassion required to survive front-line conflict.

Thus, his desire to build a remote sanctuary to escape the looming third World War, reflected Hatch's disappointment with the path human civilization was taking. Totally opposed to Hatch's plan to bug out to his cabin, his wife Shirley, a popular hairdresser with a wide customer following, gave him the ultimatum he was dreading—it was either Shirley or the cabin.

Hatch chose the cabin.

My back was sore and the muscles in my legs reminded me painfully that they were still there after considerable lack of use. Much older now, I had unfortunately slacked off my physical activities and was in poor shape for this type of strenuous activity. However, I was proud of my progress this day, laying out my tent and starting my cook fire beside the small creek that had been my goal.

I had primarily packed freeze-dried meals that were easy to carry and cook, involving minimal cleanup as well. I filled my small pot with water from the creek and set it to boil on a light, old oven grill that I had found in a junkyard many years before. With rocks carefully placed around the small fire, I had a platform for the grill to rest on in a fairly level fashion.

After eating the tasty stew, I poured some of the hot water into a mug and waited for it to cool down prior to drinking. Sadly, water in these mountain wilderness areas was no longer safe for drinking and had to be boiled or otherwise purified. Various diseases including giardia had invaded the water supply of these far-flung pristine areas, causing serious illness and even death to those who drank the clear, crisp, seemingly harmless water straight from the creek. I had an important mission to accomplish and no plans to die right now.

On the third day in the late afternoon, I faced a steep climb up from a valley to Hatch's cabin next to a little lake he dubbed "Sanctuary Lake." Hatch told me to attach a bell to my pack as I neared his cabin so he didn't mistake me for a bear or human intruder. Highly paranoid after his combat experiences, Hatch didn't really trust anyone except his friends.

Coming over a small ridge I looked around Sanctuary Lake for Hatch's cabin but could not see any building in the vicinity. I pulled out my Nikon super zoom camera and ranged it along the shoreline around the lake. Still not finding anything, I decided to walk around the lake and was about halfway back to my starting point when I heard a loud shout nearby. I looked in the direction of the sound but did not see anything until a green bush emerged from behind a screen of trees. It was Hatch in the camouflage ghillie suit he made with local vegetation attached to a breathable fabric, enabling him to blend in perfectly with ground cover in the area.

"Hey Hatch," I said, "You are a hard man to find." Hatch grabbed my hand in a crushing handshake and hugged me, lifting me with my pack up in the air and shaking me as a grizzly would shake its prey before killing it with a single bite to the neck. "Plug, you made it, my man, how was the trip?"

"Well, Hatch, it was interesting to say the least. You have picked a fine spot to hide out here. By the way, where is your cabin?"

I followed Hatch through the bush until we came to a flat shelf overlooking the lake, circled by trees with a meadow in the middle. Hatch walked into the meadow, knelt down, and pulled at something on the ground. Immediately a metal hatch came up, and I looked into the dark abyss, where a ladder was attached to one side of the narrow tunnel.

Hatch motioned me to climb down the ladder and said, "Welcome to my crib." About twenty feet down a large room opened up, lit by an LED bulb attached to the ceiling. Carved out of solid rock, the room contained a narrow cot, an electric stove for cooking, and a collection of books in a large sealed glass case container with a dehumidifier in the bottom.

Fanatical about preserving his books, Hatch knew it was best to keep books in a dry environment at about 35 percent relative humidity. A wall-mounted wooden shelving unit with dishes and dried rice and meat and other preserved foodstuffs, stood over a small sink linked to a plastic water pipe snaking up the wall and out of sight.

Hatch pulled out a bottle of homemade mountain flower wine, gave me a glass, and toasted, "Here's to ya," while we clinked glasses. As we drank the wine, I asked how he powered his true-to-life man cave. "Well, Plug, here is how I did it. There is a little stream up the hill from here, where I installed a small turbine power generator that provides me with about five kilowatts of power during the warmer months and varied lesser amounts of power after the big freeze-up comes. I also get my water from this creek."

"My waste and toilet water go out that pipe over there to a small septic field lower than this room. The waste is filtered out in the septic field and any water that makes it down to the lake is clean. I also have a latrine about one hundred feet from here that I use when I am outside. And, contrary to politically correct environmental thinking, I burn all plastic. In my view, the tiny amount of plastic biodegradable ash residue that goes into the atmosphere is less of a problem than the greater volume of non-biodegradable plastic left on the ground or in the water.

"Or, let's put it another way," Hatch continued. "If all the millions of tons of plastic floating around in our oceans was replaced by the residue left after burning this material, what would be worse, a ton of non-burnt plastic bottles or twenty-five pounds of plastic ash residue?"

"The real challenge was installing my solar panels so they could not be seen from the air. Solar panels need to face directly into the sunlight without anything blocking the sun's rays. Fortunately I was able to order green-colored solar panels and then attached curved pieces around the outside of the main square panels. As you know, there are no straight lines in nature. The bright metal framing of the panels I painted green."

Looking around the rock walls of the man-made cave, I wondered how Hatch could have carved this room from solid granite. "Oh, that was easy. With my military demolitions training and C4 explosives, I blasted the rock out the side of the hill, then filled the open side with rocks, dirt, and timber framing, covering it with soil so that natural grasses could grow back in."

"You must be hungry," Hatch said, putting some water on to boil and getting some brown rice and dried meat and vegetables off a shelf. He refilled my glass with wine and told me to rope my pack down the tunnel before bears ripped it apart.

After a hearty meal and a few more glasses of wine, Hatch suggested we go outside and enjoy the sunset. When we climbed out of the tunnel, the sun was just dipping over the horizon casting a golden glow around the lake. At this altitude, there were few mosquitoes and a paltry number of horseflies and other annoying flying bugs.

"Why did you come here?" said Hatch. "We haven't seen each other in years and have barely kept in touch."

"Well, Hatch, I need your help with a project I am working on," I said. "You have the creativity, skills, and balls to handle the operational side of Eye 1."

I quickly described the project to Hatch and he let out a huge gasp before saying, "You really are crazy, Plug. Where did you get a mad idea like this? It is beyond anything I have ever heard."

I let out a sigh and responded, "Hatch, I thought you told me you would never take another life, only saving and protecting lives when you could. This idea could potentially save thousands of lives of people adversely affected by hurricanes and other extreme weather around the globe. And with global warming advancing across the planet, these weather events are getting wilder and wilder."

"Plug," Hatch replied, "I haven't left this cabin in sixteen years, except to get mail and obtain food supplies. I am done with the world, women, and everything that goes along with it. Mark my words, hell is going to break loose any time and I will be sitting pretty up here."

Hatch seemed entrenched in his thinking, so I suggested we take a walk down to the lake. A narrow gravelly beach surrounded the outlet of the creek Hatch got his power from, abutting the sharp, rocky shoreline around the rest of the lake. The lake was only three quarters of a mile long and half a mile wide, but was several hundred feet deep, allowing a small trout population to survive the severe winters here.

I asked him how his daughters were doing these days. "They are grown up now with kids of their own. I haven't gone to see them since I moved up here and they've never been here to visit me," Hatch sadly reflected.

"That is easily explained, Hatch," I said. "This place is harder to get to than the moon. Are you on good terms with your daughters now?"

"No," Hatch said. "They still blame me for abandoning them after their mother divorced me. Also, they don't understand my hermit doomsdayer lifestyle."

"What are they doing now?" I asked.

"Both Alexandra and Elena live in Key West, Florida, with their families. Both of them run a bar there with Ernest, Elena's husband. Alexandra got divorced a few years ago and has custody of her son Jake. Elena has two kids, a girl and a boy."

With darkness gathering around us, we sauntered back up to Hatch's underground home and dug into the wine again, before settling in for the night at about nine.

I awoke early the next morning, stirred by a rapping sound outside. I climbed the ladder, opened the hatch, and found Hatch chopping up a deadfall that had fallen recently near his underground chamber. "I am surprised you have any fires up here," I said. "I thought you didn't want to tip off anybody that you are here."

"That's right," Hatch replied. "I only use very dry woods that burn cleanly and give off little smoke. Also, I wait until there is a breeze off the mountain that carries the smoke down laterally through the trees, fizzling out and dispersing it at the base of the valley, where tiny white puffs of smoke rise into the air that could be mistaken as steam or fog off the creek."

"Would you like some breakfast," Hatch asked. "I've got some trout I can fry up and some excellent homemade bread I made myself." Hatch put a pot of coffee on the stove and started frying the trout on an old cast iron pan he had found in an abandoned trapper's shack dating back one hundred years or more.

"What would you like to do today?" he said. "We can take a look around the area if you want."

"Well, Hatch," I said, "I seem to remember you mentioning a natural hot spring you found around here. I'd like to take a look at it and have a good soak."

Natural hot springs are prevalent in western Canada and western United States, formed from deep volcanic activity that causes red hot magma to rise and heat waters close to the surface that bubble out of the ground at high temperatures. This creates a perfect opportunity for bathing in these healthful, mineral-rich waters.

"That's fine. I'll pack a bag of sandwiches and a jug of wine and we will be on our way," Hatch replied.

It turned out to be a steep two-hour climb from Hatch's cabin through a stand of spindly subalpine fir trees, where we reached a false summit and gazed up at the snowcapped peak several thousand feet above us. We took in the spectacular view for a minute before angling along the side of the mountain toward a steep drop we could see several miles away.

Reaching the precipice, we looked down through trees toward a small creek with steam rising in clouds from a pool directly below us. Sliding down the slope with the backs of our boots dug into the dirt in proper glissading fashion, Hatch yelled out, "Yippee kioh!" as we rocketed to the bottom, where a large log blocked our path. We managed to break our fall by grabbing onto bushes and digging our boots even further into the ground. Coming to a stop immediately in front of the log, we sprang over the log barely touching it with our hands as if we were jumping over a pommel horse in a gym.

We dropped our packs as I studied the small man-made pool that had been created with large rocks set in concrete to prevent any leaks. "Someone must have had a horse or mule to haul this concrete up here," I told Hatch.

"No, this brush is too thick and terrain too steep for any packhorse or burro to make it in here," he replied. "Some tough son of a bitch packed the concrete in on his back."

Further examining the slightly inclined area around the pool, I noticed a plastic pipe entering the pool on the high side, the other end of the thirty-foot pipe joined in sections and laid nimbly into a small natural spring above where hot water combined with cold creek water before draining into the hot pool below. My guess was that the hot spring water was about 180 degrees Fahrenheit at the source, and after mixing with creek water the resulting liquid plunged into the pool about 105 F, at the outer limits of what people can safely stand.

We stripped off our clothes and slowly immersed ourselves in the sulphur-smelling water, propping our wine jug on a flattish rock at the edge of the pool.

Hatch took a few pulls from the jug and said, "So, what do you think of it, Plug, is it hot enough for you?"

"Plenty hot," I replied. "Any hotter and my crown jewels will be boiled like a Bavarian sausage."

We floated around in the pool for a while, occasionally pulling our upper bodies out of the water to cool off, before re-immersing ourselves in the soothing liquid.

Hatch described what it was like for him to live

up here all year long. "When I first started working for the forest service after I got out of the Navy, they offered me the job of being a fire lookout and I grabbed the opportunity, thinking that peace and quiet would do me good."

A forestry lookout mans a tower on top of a mountain that allows unhampered viewing of all points of the compass, and is charged with the task of spotting wildfires and radioing in their locations to fire crews nearby. A lonely job with lots of downtime unless it is a very active fire season, few people can handle the isolation and not many people apply for the job. In recent years, lookout towers have been replaced by plane overflights and satellites. There are even drones constantly monitoring forest conditions and identifying fires in their early stages of development, enabling rapid deployment of firefighting resources to the hotspot.

The famous author, Jack Kerouac, who wrote the well-known *On the Road*, published in 1957, spent sixty-three days as a fire lookout in 1956, thinking he could write up there amidst the peace and solitude. However, that plan didn't work out for Kerouac who missed all the earthly pleasures he was used to, including people, drugs, alcohol, and women, not necessarily in that order. As for writing, Kerouac barely managed to pen a few Haikus and a letter to his mother, before being recalled from his post due to his tendency to turn the radio off so he could write.

A book titled *Desolation Angels*, published in 1960, recalled Kerouac's forest lookout experiences but his signature classic, *On the Road*, became the anthem for the beat generation and helped inspire the hippie movement of the 1960s and 1970s.

Hatch's summer on the forestry tower was quite different than Jack Kerouac's services in that position. "I totally loved the solitude and did quite a bit of reading and nature study during that time. I also conducted early experiments in brewing mountain wine, which I hid from my supervisor who came in once by horse to restock my supplies and check on how I was doing. He thought I was a little weird in my habits but was happy with my performance on the job."

"The big event that summer was a lightning strike that started a fire in a pine forest about five miles from the tower, quickly advancing through dry brush before a smokejumper crew was dropped into the remote location to try and snuff it out. Unfortunately, the wind-fueled inferno was moving too quickly up the slope for firefighters, who had to be pulled out by helicopter before they were burnt to a crisp.

"The fire continued for another day, moving toward my location with thick smoke covering the tower, preventing any visibility from my perch.

Heavy rains the next day quelled the fire, which had torched the bush to a point about one mile below my lookout. The fire had been left to burn out naturally, given the poor quality timber and lack of any people or buildings in the area."

Our skin turning pruny as if we had been poached like an egg, Hatch and I decided to get out of the pool to eat our sandwiches, washed down by some wine. Mellowed by the long soak, we were both in a reflective mood, the talk turning back to my scheme.

"I've been thinking about your project and am willing to help in any way I can," Hatch said. "I think it is a worthwhile step in the process of preserving the planet and saving lives as well as improving our understanding of global warming. Plus, I think it will be a hoot and a big adrenaline rush, something I haven't had for a while."

"Ok," I said. "You're on."

Chapter Eight
Up, Up and Away

After I got back home from my visit with Hatch, my enthusiasm for Eye 1 was rekindled anew, stimulating fresh ideas for securing our funding and completion of our recruitment for the Eye 1 crew.

I checked on our crowd-funding post to see how much we had raised so far, and my heart dropped when I saw the number on my Macintosh computer screen—$16,224. This amount was barely enough to fly to the ocean and get wet, much less launch a brand new submersible with unique capabilities. I speculated that people looking at the Eye 1 post probably thought it was a scam or hoax to raid people's pocketbooks. I talked to Hatch and he commiserated with me about the situation, suggesting that maybe we should get more publicity for the project, raising our profile in the public eye, thereby gaining more credibility with potential funding sources.

"Yes, Hatch, you may be on to something there, I

51

will give it a try," I said.

A reporter at a daily newspaper in the 1970s, I was very handy at writing up press releases and made short work of an article describing the Eye 1 project. I focused on the fact that an Eye 1 reality show would capture the imagination of TV viewers while offering something worthwhile that had never been done before. Also, I posted the article on various social media including Facebook and Twitter.

There was virtually no response to the article in the local paper until the major news services picked up the story and disseminated it all over the print and electronic media, including *The New York Times* — online and print — Google News, and many other popular online news feeds.

I started getting calls seeking interviews and inviting me on various TV talk shows and news outlets. My first interview on CNN's *Larry King Live* didn't go very well. Larry and his viewers peppered me with all kinds of questions about my legitimacy, background, and capability to deliver on a project like this. I fired back with, "The largest tree grows from a single seed, the longest journey begins with a single step, and if you don't try, failure is a certainty."

The more shows and interviews I did, the better I became at explaining the Eye 1 idea, and the more contacts I made. People I hadn't seen in years phoned me with encouragement for the project and affirmed my character as a no-nonsense, no bullshit, trustworthy person.

Prominent people invited me into their homes and clubs and offered assistance, financial and otherwise, to get the project going. Even the Explorer Society, based in New York, asked me to give a talk to their members, endorsing my project in a unanimous vote. Their membership included Jim Cameron and Bob Ballard, both well-known ocean explorers, with Ballard finding the Titanic and other historical wrecks, and Cameron doing the deepest solo dive with a mini-sub and producing the box office record-breaking movie, *Titanic*, in the 1990s.

The key selling point to my pitch was that I wasn't out to personally profit from Eye 1, but rather planned to set up a nonprofit organization overseen by a blue ribbon board with many audit oversight checks and balances. Too many charitable organizations had been discredited in recent years with accusations of greed and mismanagement involving principals of these groups.

I intended to be completely transparent with Eye 1, posting the audited books online with regular updates and information. And I vowed that 100 percent of donated funds and revenue from the reality show would go toward the project with no administration fees. This pledge was made possible due to the backing of a prominent billionaire who said he would cover all administration costs and voluntarily serve on the Eye 1 board.

When I first met the billionaire known as "The Sage of Sacramento" in his New York office, he looked me over carefully and said, "I normally don't support environmental causes like this, but I'm very worried about global warming and its negative consequences affecting the economy, jobs, people, and the environment. Upsetting the global applecart is bad business for everyone. Further, I think there will be useful peaceful spin-offs from this new technology that will not only aid the environment but encourage international cooperation and goodwill meshed with advancing the world economy."

Mr. Soffit was very funny, laughing when I said I thought he was the creator of those famous insurance company ads featuring the small lizard with a British accent. "No, I have nothing to do with those ads," he said with a twinkle in his eye. "We have an ad agency that comes up with that stuff." When queried about how he made all his money, Soffit replied, "Value investing was the key, buying undervalued brands with unique niches in the market and holding them over an extended time period."

When I suggested I knew how he really made these large returns, Mr. Soffit bristled and said, "What do you mean?" I responded, "Mr. Soffit, I know you are a math and probabilities genius. What you have done is assemble a boiler room of the best minds in math, business, stock markets, insurance actuarial calculations, world economics, tax law, and a variety of other money-related subdisciplines. With these top-of-the food chain minds along with a couple of supercomputers and your peerless business intelligence-gathering staff, you are able to calculate and predict where to move your money and resources for the greatest returns at any given time. Unlike any other investor, you know exactly when to sell ice to Eskimos for the largest return."

The modest Sage of Sacramento scoffed at my assertions. "I am just a genial 'aw shucks!' folk hero who plays the fiddle occasionally. I'm the same as anyone else and just got lucky. Anyone can do what I have done. It was just hard work and nothing else."

Leaving his office, I thanked Mr. S for his support of Eye 1 and said, "I've always been a fan. As a small business owner it is hard enough to stay afloat, but your accomplishments are mind-boggling."

My wife, Honeybunch, supported Eye 1, but was glad I kept working at my small building management business while organizing the Eye 1 project. However, she was greatly concerned about my safety in the tiny sub getting thrashed around in the eye of a hurricane. "You are taking a big risk, Plug," she said. "I would hate to lose you." I comforted her with, "We are going about this carefully and methodically, ensuring every precaution is taken to protect the safety of the crew. Plus, we are planning to stock every kind of sea sickness pill and related item to minimize the barf factor."

Honeybunch had learned to deal with my eccentricities and off the wall behavior that had led me down many strange and wonderful paths. "I never wanted to be a 'cookie cutter' person," I said, "copying and imitating what everyone around me did. In my view, the history of civilization is the story of the masses coupled with individual actions and ideas that propelled knowledge forward. These creative people were the geese that laid the golden eggs, leaving their cookie-cutter compatriots in the dust. But, in defense of the nameless legions of the body politic, without their bland conformism, Einstein and others would not have distinguished themselves so greatly. Without ying, you cannot have yang."

I sent a letter off to Hatch describing the progress we made and asking him to send a list of the kind of people we needed to round out the crew. My thinking was that we would need a meteorologist, an engineer, a communications expert, a doctor, and a few other highly skilled professionals.

I contacted Arch and asked him to start working on the actual design of Eye 1 as I put together the sponsorship of the project and found a TV producer to organize the Eye 1 reality show and find a network to distribute it.

CHAPTER NINE
TRACTION

With all my appearances in the media and the confidence I was gaining as a result, I continued to call potential sponsors and meet with them, outlining the purposes of Eye 1 and pointing out that Eye 1 would be the genesis of new meteorological technology and spin-off vessels that could complement its groundbreaking research work.

Just like NASA (United States National Aeronautics and Space Administration) had accomplished in the last 50+ years, many new technologies needed for the space program ended up being very useful for solving many earthbound problems, including memory foam, freeze-dried food, firefighting equipment, emergency space blankets, dust-busters, Cochlear implants, and Speedo's LZR Razor swimsuits. NASA says there are over 1,650 other spin-offs in the fields of computer technology, environment and agriculture, health and medicine, public safety, transportation, recreation, and industrial productivity. Contrary to popular belief, NASA did not invent Teflon, Tang or Velcro.

Eye 1 could be the same kind of technology incubator as the space program, justifying the huge development costs of this new super-sub. And, unlike many donations to charities which often go down a bottomless hole, Eye 1 sponsors could separately invest in and advance these new technologies.

Once I reined in enough sponsors to create the large development fund necessary for Eye 1, I organized a meeting of all these individuals and entities. The National Weather Service, part of the National Oceanic and Atmospheric Administration (NOAA), provided the venue for the meeting at no cost at their National Hurricane Center offices in Florida.

The purpose of the two-day meeting was to set up the nonprofit charter of the Eye 1 organization, discuss details of the project, and work out a tentative plan for implementation of Eye 1 including establishment of a working group to oversee the development process.

After convening the meeting, I looked out at the faces of the several hundred people gathered there, my heart swelling with the realization that these people believed in me and our mission, that getting a better handle on extreme weather patterns and climate change, provided hope for the planet's well-being.

Chatting with sponsors and other supporters of Eye 1 during the lunch breaks and social events, including a banquet and outdoor barbecue, redoubled my enthusiasm for what we were doing. Also in attendance was a well-known reality show producer with a sterling track record for hit TV shows, considered "The Dean" of his TV genre. His world-class beautiful Irish wife Shannon, a TV star in her own right, bedazzled the crowd with her poise and charm, sharp as a tack with her in-depth understanding of the project.

"Plug," Shannon said, "I know you are not a religious man but you have to agree there is a divine hand in this mission, that it will not succeed without the Holy Father's blessing and support."

I responded with, "I am an agnostic with an open mind about the presence of a supernatural being, requiring irrefutable evidence that he or she actually exists. With all the bad things happening in the world, I am presently skeptical about the existence of this divine entity. However, I will be very happy if you prove me wrong, and you are welcome to lead the religious arm of our organization. We need all the help we can get."

After the meeting, a hive of activity commenced in all aspects of the Eye 1 project. Arch worked with other architects and engineers to finalize vessel design, sponsors negotiated the specifics of their funding arrangements, and Hatch worked with me to find other volunteers to man the new boat.

Hatch moved into the little shed beside our house that was equipped with a stove, fridge, bathroom, bed, and not much else. Hatch worked out every spare minute available and I went partway with him on his afternoon runs. A former pro boxer, Hatch regularly ran 20+ mile runs, and I was able to do the first five miles barely keeping up with him. He continued on for an hour and a half after that, completing a large road circuit back to our house.

We put the word out on social media and our website that we were looking for volunteers for the Eye 1 project, people with very special skills in their chosen professions. Pretty soon Hatch and I were reviewing hundreds of applications, most online, that poured in for the small number of crew positions available on the sub.

"I can't believe the quality level of most of these applications," Hatch said. "I don't think we are going to have a problem finding the people we need. The main challenge will be to sign up crewmembers with the right temperaments who work well with other people and take direction."

With his Navy background, I decided that Hatch would be the captain of the vessel and I would take the role of onboard coordinator of the mission, deferring to Hatch on matters related to boat operation and safety.

My task would be to execute mission goals and strategy that were being determined by our expert working group, which included National Weather Service advisors that zeroed in on data they were lacking to improve hurricane models and prediction techniques. Understanding more about hurricanes and other extreme weather phenomena would enable weather and climate agencies to save more lives and reduce property and infrastructure damage. Knowledge is power.

Our first interviewee was a quiet, short man with a mop of thick red hair. His understated personality belied his vast engineering experience in all mechanical and technological aspects of ocean-going vessels, large and small. His name, Sean Campbell, reflected his Scottish roots, his Scots accent coming through clearly as he explained his background and great desire to be part of the Eye 1 project.

"I don't have any experience with this new supercavitation technology, but I'm a quick learner if I can work with the design engineers while they are building this boat," Campbell said. "I may have a few ideas they can incorporate in this vessel based on my experiences as an engineer on nuclear subs."

Hatch and I deliberated briefly in an adjacent

room in our hastily rented temporary headquarters, a former mattress store, while Sean waited in my office. Hatch said, "I think he is the man we want, Plug. Sean's credentials are head and shoulders above anyone else we have interviewed."

"I agree," I replied. "He's our man."

The next candidate we chose was a female meteorologist from Atlanta, Georgia. With a PhD in meteorology, Angela Murdoch had been on many research expeditions around the world and distinguished herself with groundbreaking papers on global warming and its climatic and weather implications.

On looking over her prominent curves and drop-dead gorgeous appearance, I asked her if she had ever been on TV, as I thought I had seen her on TV once a long time ago. "Yes, for a short time after I got out of college I worked as a CNN meteorologist, but quickly got bored as it was repetitive and superficial, not really delving in depth into weather or climate phenomena."

The remainder of the crew, a computer expert and a doctor, were chosen quickly, several of them having multiple skills to bring to the mix. The doctor, Doc Ozz, was also an experienced deep-sea diver and the computer expert, Harry Hackbarth, aka Hack, a former Microsoft employee, had the rare ability to modify and adapt technology on the spot in crisis situations.

Hack had been instrumental in correcting the flaws in the botched Obamacare website which had bombed in its initial rollout, most people totally frustrated in their attempts to get affordable health care. President Obama had never made a website and assumed it was an easier process than it turned out to be. Also, the Secretary of Health and Human Services, Kathleen Sebelius, wasn't hands-on enough to ensure proper rollout of the groundbreaking affordable care act.

Our crew assembled, we began training for our operations on Eye 1, familiarizing ourselves with our mission and objectives, as well as getting used to each other and learning to work as a team.

Part of our training was getting ourselves physically fit to handle the rigors of ocean research work in the hellish conditions of extreme maritime weather events. Hatch led our physical training, pushing us to the very limits of our capabilities. Push-ups, sit-ups, weight training, running, swimming, and use of diving gear were a few of the grueling activities he put us through.

"Are you trying to kill me?" Sean shouted at Hatch as he tried to stay afloat while Hatch grabbed him and pulled him underwater, replicating part of Navy Seal training where they learn to rescue people panicking after being tossed into the sea when their boat goes down.

Sean struggled to the surface and managed to get his arm around Hatch and pull him backward toward the pool edge with strong kicking strokes. "The ocean will give you no quarter, Sean, you can't be a pussy in these situations," Hatch responded.

Angela was an excellent swimmer and diver, the male crewmembers' most popular partner in the various water training scenarios. "Quit groping me, Hatch," she screamed, exasperated. Hatch let her surface after holding her under water, her blond hair draped over her mask, confusing her further. "You did well, Angela," Hatch replied, pulling his mask down and smiling at her broadly. "I can't very well do this exercise without touching you."

A good chemistry was developing between Hatch and Angela, recovering after a bitter divorce with her pro football husband Joe, whose philandering ways earned him the nickname "Hollywood Joe." They parted with no children involved, Angela in her mid-30s ready to have a family and be a mom. Coming from a close-knit southern family, Angela was anxious to wind down her high energy career and focus on bringing up the next generation.

Doc Ozz excelled at the swimming and diving training, and could do four laps of the pool under water. Ozz was a loner, never having gotten married and a workaholic, intensely working around the clock when a particular crisis needed to be resolved. He was an emergency room doctor who regularly volunteered to help in disasters around the world, including the earthquake in Haiti and the Fukushima tsunami and nuclear plant meltdown in Japan.

I met frequently with Arch and his staff as he coordinated the design and construction of Eye 1, relying on a network of high-tech wizards determined to make this revolutionary new technology work. The key design element of the Eye 1 vessel was the supercavitation technology, where small prototypes were fleshing out operational characteristics of the propulsion system at a special long test pool at the Massachusetts Institute of Technology.

As I watched a prototype test run, the tiny sub hesitated for a brief second before rocketing to the other end of the pool at a blinding speed barely discernible to the naked eye. A special series of nets at the other end of the pool reduced its speed so it didn't crash into the wall. The speed was clocked at 60 mph which would increase to over 100 mph in the full size completed Eye 1. One of the primary concerns of the designers was the effect Eye 1 would have on the undersea ecosystem as it travelled along at record speeds.

"We are confident the gas bubble created in front of Eye 1 will push away fish and plant life in advance of the vessel so that no life-forms will be harmed by the sub," said Arch. "We have inserted fish and plants in the pool and nothing has been damaged so far. Also, when we do the sea trials of Eye 1, we will place instruments along the test route which will measure any ecosystem damage. Of course, garbage and other materials floating on the ocean surface won't pose any problem as we will mostly travel several hundred feet under water."

"How deep will she be able to go?" I asked Arch. "We expect to go to the bottom of the deepest trenches in the world's oceans, including the Mariana Trench in the western Pacific Ocean, the deepest ocean trench in the world at 36,000 feet," said Arch.

"The first mission to the deepest point at the bottom of the Mariana Trench, called the Challenger Deep, was in 1960 by the US Navy bathyscaphe Trieste manned by Don Walsh and Jacques Piccard," Arch continued. Several unmanned descents followed which were superseded by James Cameron's record solo descent of the Mariana Trench when he spent three hours exploring the ocean floor with high-tech sampler arms and video equipment specially designed for the craft."

"Jim Cameron has given us special permission to study the unique technology used in the design of *Deepsea Challenger* including a new type of syntactic foam, called Isofloat, that compensates for the huge compressive forces at 6.8 miles deep."

CHAPTER TEN
TV SHOW

The reality TV producer who volunteered to make a reality show out of our Eye 1 project invited me to visit the set of one of his reality show hits, *Survival*, a long-running show involving individuals competing for a $1,000,000 prize given to the last person standing in the competition. R.E. Allity wanted me to get a handle on how a reality show is made, so he could do the best possible job on *Eye 1*.

"Of course, the big difference between *Survival* and *Eye 1* is that *Survival* is a kind of contrived reality whereas *Eye 1* will be actual reality with all the starkness, unpredictability and danger associated with putting a cutting-edge submersible into wildly dangerous waters," said R.E. "Thus, we will not be in control of most of what happens."

The *Survival* set was a hive of activity as contestants milled around the camp performing their daily chores while meeting in small groups

68

and individually to carry out their various plans and conspiracies designed to eliminate other participants from the competition.

"R.E., to be frank, I have never really understood this show," I said. "In my experience working for the forest service and participating in outdoor activities, we were trained to work as a team and look out for our teammates. It was one for all and all for one. Your show is the opposite of this."

"Well, Plug," R.E. replied, "this is showbiz and we want to get our ratings as high as possible. If contestants on the show were always sweet and nice and cooperative, nobody would watch it. High drama and conflict are essential to our winning formula."

Camera crews were located everywhere on the set including in the palm trees to film every twitch and turn of the participants. Additionally, small remote cameras picked up any action missed by the camera operators. Hundreds of hours were filmed, then carefully edited and distilled into the one-hour weekly shows.

I spoke to a few of the contestants including Zooey, a tiny well-shaped woman bursting with energy and exuberance. Zooey was considered one of the power players on the show, manipulating and coercing her counterparts with a subtle charm that put them at ease while ensnaring them in her web of deceit.

"I have been watching this show for years and have picked up on winning strategies and techniques that keep you in the game until the end," said Zooey. "It is a delicate dance with few missteps allowed." In real life Zooey was a psychologist, the show giving her the perfect opportunity to display her in-depth understanding of human behavior, with a million dollar carrot dangling at the end of the session.

R.E. was in his element supervising the production, his military training enabling him to command and coordinate the chaotic situation with the smoothness and assurance of a master. With so many reality shows in production at the same time, R.E. had to apportion his time very carefully, popping in to each set on a regular basis to tune up and adjust show content to optimize entertainment values.

"*Eye 1* will be a reality show production in a class by itself," R.E. said. "The immense challenges of filming on a submarine will require advanced technology and techniques to capture the action on the vessel. We will have to up our game considerably to make this show work. You and your crew will have to get used to the intrusiveness of the TV production teams as you carry out Eye 1's missions."

CHAPTER ELEVEN
HOME

Back at home I went on a run with Hatch and reviewed progress on the project. We had secured our funding and were on track to build Eye 1 on schedule, ready to go on its sea trials in two months.

Training of the crew was going well with Hatch whipping his colleagues into shape physically and a team of high tech and sub experts familiarizing the crew with the state-of-the-art technology built into the very seams of Eye 1.

Consultations with the National Hurricane Center and other weather experts were regularly updating us on forecasts for the upcoming hurricane season which was going to be a doozy, with many major storms predicted that could supersede the destructive force of other record seasons.

"Everything is going well, Plug," Hatch said, barely puffing as we ran up a steep hill. "The crewmembers are jelling and our technical advisors are doing a bang-up job of bringing the crew up to speed on these new technologies. We are going to kick some ass."

"How is Angela doing?" I asked. "Angela is doing great," Hatch said. "We even had a few beers together and did some dancing. She is a perfect ten in my book with mind and body to match. Angela is clueing me in on how these superstorms work and the kind of data we need to collect when we are in the middle of one of these things. It was all Greek to me as we didn't deal with studying hurricanes in the seals, however, we were careful about checking the forecast prior to embarking on any mission."

CHAPTER TWELVE
THE REAL DEAL

I phoned Arch and he said construction of Eye 1 was on schedule at the Electric Boat Company shipyards in Groton, Connecticut, where most of the early nuclear submarines were built. "It is a real challenge for them to build this unique new craft," Arch said. "They have their best engineers working on it along with a team of experts from the Eye 1 working group. Scaling the design from the small models tested at MIT is very difficult given that not all design features of Eye 1 perform the same at the model level compared to the full-sized sub."

I invited Arch to meet me in Groton in a couple of days to review progress on Eye 1. We had visited the boatyard several times when they began construction of Eye 1 and were excited to see the progress made on our "baby." Also, the rest of the crew including Hatch were going to be there to get briefed on the status of the project and examine the unfolding reality of Eye

1. The crew needed to be intimately acquainted with every aspect of Eye 1's design and construction, so that in the event of problems developing, they would be best equipped to handle these situations.

Eye 1's crew stayed at the Best Western in Groton and we got together at the bar to catch up with each other prior to heading out to Electric Boat the next morning. Hatch and Angela were already sitting at the bar when I got there and I sat down next to them, ordering a Samuel Adams lager draft beer for myself, a fresh Tequila Sunrise for Angela, and another Jack Daniels for Hatch. They greeted me heartily and we joked about the physical training program Hatch was putting everyone through. "I have never been this fit in my life," Angela said. "I have lost fifteen pounds and can run a mile in five minutes and twenty seconds. If I can keep this up I will never have to go on a diet again. Hatch is a fanatic with this stuff."

"I want her to look as good as possible," Hatch countered. "Being the only woman onboard, she has to keep our morale up."

"You sexist bastard," Angela replied. "You are old and wrinkly and full of bullshit. I don't know why I put up with you."

"Because I am so sweet and lovable," said Hatch.

The rest of the crew came in and we moved to a big table. Hack and Ozz ordered double Alaskan Everclear 190 overproof shots while Sean asked for a glass of milk. "Are you some kind of pussy, Sean, not having a man's drink?" Hack said. "I like to have my wits about me at all times," responded Sean. "You guys better not drink on the boat."

"There will be no drinking on Eye 1," I quickly interjected.

The British Navy abolished their "tot of rum" ration in 1970 after ongoing problems with tipsy sailors performing poorly at their stations.

The British Navy rum ration traditionally consisted of seventy milliliters of rum given to every sailor at midday. The rum ration was usually served from one barrel, known as the "rum tub," ornately decorated and reinforced with brass. When boarding their ship, sailors were asked if they were members of the Temperance Movement. If they replied in the affirmative, it was noted in the ship's records and they were given three pence a day instead of rum. The Up Spirits rum ration was distributed between eleven a.m. and twelve noon. Sailors under twenty were not permitted any rum.

Hack was full of piss and vinegar and ready to head out to sea today, if he could. "I'm fed up with this waiting," Hack said. "We pretty much have all the computer equipment ready to go and I have designed special software for our navigation system so that we can go pretty much anywhere, to any depth. I have integrated all the latest navigation and communications technology including sonar, GPS, acoustic transmission, very low frequency, and standard surface radio transmission via satellites into one pod. I then made two more pods which will provide second and third levels of system redundancy with backup power for all."

"Surface radio communication will be easy and we will use very low frequency radio waves when we are in shallow depths up to twenty meters," Hack said. Also, we will deploy a buoy on a long cable from Eye 1 equipped with an antenna that rises to a few meters above the surface to extend our underwater VLF range."

"For really deep situations, we have received special permission from the US Navy to use their acoustic transmission system which involves underwater speakers and hydrophones," Hack explained. "The US Navy has placed sonic communication equipment in the seabed of areas frequently traveled by their submarines and connected it by underwater cables to their land stations. If a submarine submerges near one of these devices, it can stay in contact with headquarters."

I asked Doc Ozz how medical preparations were going. "Plug, I think I will be as prepared as I can be, given that I have never practiced medicine on a deep-sea submarine, "Ozz said. "With the help of Hack, we created a number of health data sensors that will be attached to crewmembers' bodies with real-time streaming of health data to our supercomputers. The computers will instantaneously examine the data for problems including heart rate, blood pressure, traumas, and other health concerns and relay the information to my Apple Watch with alerts if any crewmember's health and well-being is compromised. This way I can take fast action if anyone is in trouble."

"Also, we are ready to test special exoskeletons the crew can wear to provide them with greater strength and speed in dicey situations," Doc said. "The exoskeletons can be fitted with dive gear and special re-breather oxygen units that will enable these six million dollar super divers make Jacques Cousteau, the famous deep-sea explorer and inventor of the Aqua-Lung in the 1940s, look like a minnow attached to a sea turtle. We are expecting underwater speeds of twenty to twenty-five mph from divers equipped with this cutting-edge equipment."

"Great," I said. "We are going to push the envelope of technology in every respect on Eye 1, and I believe we will come up with more new technologies as the project proceeds on its missions."

I then asked Sean for an update on the engineering capabilities of Eye 1. "I have a pretty good handle on the supercavitation technology and helped the design team fine-tune various characteristics of this new propulsion technology," Sean replied. "One thing we have figured out is how to adjust our speed quickly when we are switching from high-speed maneuvers to low-speed tasks. Also, we have designed special thrusters that will enable Eye 1 to move in any direction, up, down, or sideways, when it is in a stationary position or moving slowly."

"We have improved the nuclear power plant safety systems and reduced the size of the reactor," Sean said. "Likely we can easily resupply our food and equipment at various ports of call, but will carry a two-year supply of food onboard in case we need it. A hydroponic vegetable growing unit will allow us to grow some of our fruits and vegetables on the vessel. Given that we have a relatively small crew, cabin space needed is at a minimum, which frees up space for the hydroponic garden and other activities.

"We have optimized our use of space with design features controlled by software that enables walls and other internal equipment to be moved to accommodate our various missions," Sean continued. "Helping this process is the amazing strength of the syntactic foam hull support that requires less internal structural reinforcement than conventional submarines."

CHAPTER THIRTEEN
CHOW

We ordered another round of drinks while we viewed the menus for our dinner. Arch ordered a double martini shaken not stirred, while the rest of us put in our dinner orders. Hatch ordered a big T-bone steak with all the trimmings, Angela requested a chef salad, Sean went with corned beef and hagus, a Scottish delicacy, while Doc Ozz and I put in for a big bowl of beef stew. Hack ordered a cheeseburger, fries, and a cherry Coke, saying, "I'm with the Sage of Sacramento, food for a three year old is just fine for me."

With the entire Eye 1 crew present, conversation began to amp up as we started eating dinner. Unhappy with the slow pace of booze service, Hatch told the waiter to "Keep it flowing, my man, when a glass is empty fill it up immediately. I'm practically on the wagon with this slow service."

Talk centered around our goals for the Eye 1

project. "I think we should initially focus on the shakedown cruise to get our systems working smoothly and our crew to gel as a unit," I said. "We want to make sure everything is working properly before we head into a hurricane."

"But beyond the operational side of things, we need to get our mission statement clearly defined," I continued. "If we don't do this, the media will make monkeys out of us by twisting what we say to suit their news cycles and sensationalizing our efforts to up their ratings."

A former news reporter, I knew that many members of the media were opportunistic byline grabbers bent upon advancing their careers at the expense of anyone or any story that came across their paths. Lack of a social conscience coupled with mercenary motives made many reporters forget they are part of society too. Any dirt they can dig up or muck they can rake is fair game for the front page, even if it only serves their narrow immediate purposes rather than the greater good of society.

Implicit in many media members' thinking is the notion there is always a snake under every rock and conspiracies loom in every news post. To them the fourth estate is the final arbiter of everything, judge and jury for all who pass through the pearly gates. Keeping things in reasonable perspective is not part of their repertoire.

"I agree," Angela chimed in. "We must be very careful how we present ourselves to the media. The reality show will help make us more transparent to the media, and having open financial books regularly printed on our website will assist this process, but we must conduct ourselves in a professional manner at all times."

"You mean I can't take you out dancing anymore," Hatch said. Angela laughed and said, "Hatch, you won't be able to touch me anymore when people are watching, even when we are dancing. Our relationship must be strictly platonic."

Hatch patted Angela on the butt and put his arms around her, before kissing her openly on the mouth. "Like this you mean," Hatch said.

The talk turned to the high risk factor of the missions and how this will affect our families. Honeybunch and I had three boys just out of college, who had expressed concerns about why I was doing this. I told them it was something I felt compelled to do, and that I wouldn't have done it when they were younger.

"I never had much respect for mountain climbers and other daredevils with young families, who put their lives at risk on a regular basis," I said. "Risk-takers who are single are a different story as they don't have a family depending on them. Many mountain climbers have a particular selfish side to

81

their natures, evidenced by their compunction to get to the top at any cost, even if their team members fall by the wayside.

In the long scope of history, whether or not a climber made it to the top of any particular peak, is probably less relevant than the impact a climber's death had on their dependents. I have always viewed mountain climbing as essentially a solo sport, where individuals mass together to achieve a goal by necessity rather than choice. I hope Eye 1's crew will be different."

Doc Ozz, a loner with no family, spoke up. "I heartily agree with Plug. Part of my rationale for living the dangerous life I've had, is that I don't put others at risk from my own self-induced behavior."

CHAPTER FOURTEEN
LOOKING GOOD

We rose early and had a hearty breakfast before heading over to the boatyards to check progress on Eye 1.

Greeting us at the boatyard, Arch introduced us to other marine architects and engineers who were completing final touches to Eye 1. Raised up on construction supports, Eye 1 gleamed with its silver coat of paint, specially formulated to optimize boat speed and resist barnacle and bacteria growth. Barnacles can make a ship burn up to 40 percent more fuel. Their collective mass is small compared to the overall ship, but their tiny bodies have an outsized effect creating drag around the ship's otherwise smooth hull.

Biofouling is the technical name for the crusting of barnacles, mussels, and bacteria on ships. Barnacles, with their super strong non-soluble glue, are the worst problems, especially for the United States

Navy, whose vessels are docked for most of the year. The Navy spends an additional $500 million per year in fuel and maintenance costs due to biofouling. Now there are solutions to biofouling, but chemicals that kill barnacles aren't good for the ocean.

In the eighteenth century, the British Navy began sheathing their ships in copper, which made the hulls immune to both barnacles and another hazard to wooden ships of the era, shipworms. Under water, a toxic film forms on the copper, keeping away any marine life. Copper sheathing was probably one of the primary factors that contributed to the emergence of England as a naval superpower in the eighteenth century.

Copper sheathing was replaced by stronger steel ships, as the presence of copper causes steel to corrode faster. They could, however, still use copper-based paints. Other paints were also tried, using poisons such as arsenic, mercury, strychnine, cyanide, and tin which worked well but killed off everything around it. Tin-based tributyltin was banned after it killed off oyster farms in Europe.

The United States Navy had announced plans for a Robotic Hull Bio-Mimetic Underwater Grooming system, or Hull Bug. Similar to a robotic home floor cleaner or pool cleaner that are designed to be tether free, Hull Bug is autonomous and runs on batteries, serving as a four-wheeled underwater Roomba for barnacles.

Antifouling remedies easier to implement will probably come from the world of chemistry. Most recently, Argentinian scientists had found that chemicals isolated from the Maytenus tree can repel barnacles, but whether this material can handle sea conditions is still to be determined.

We walked around Eye 1 noting her clean lines and sleek appearance, before climbing up a movable stair structure to enter the vessel. The last time most of the crew had been inside Eye 1 was before the interior work had been completed. Crewmembers oohed and ahed in the command center filled with LED displays controlling and monitoring every aspect of the submarine's operations. The centerpiece of the command center was a large window at the bow end of the center, providing a front row view of the ocean for all crewmembers.

Arch stepped in and said, "It isn't a real window as no current submarine window technology could handle the immense pressures of the deepest ocean trenches. Instead, we placed a number of camera sensors on the front of the bow which are projected onto the inside supersized LED window-like screen, making it appear as if we are looking through a real window."

Two cutting-edge supercomputers, one computer a redundant backup in case the primary supercomputer went down, were located under the command center, processing data at mind-boggling speeds millions of times faster than a typical desktop computer or Smartphone. This warp speed number-crunching ability would enable us to instantly process data into 3D renderings of weather systems, storm models, and real-time surface and underwater readings, which we would transmit back to our headquarters and the National Weather Service via satellite each time we surface.

Angela would examine this data and provide her analysis, prior to more detailed review by meteorologists on land. And to top it all off, fast data analysis will dictate modifications in the type of data collected and the manner in which this information is gathered.

"We are never going to be able to create a perfect model of a hurricane system, as it is currently impossible to record all data associated with extreme weather phenomena," Angela said. "However, if we can gather 90+ percent of storm data, we have a fighting chance to create highly accurate predictive hurricane models that can save lives and limit property damage."

"Also, as our data set increases from multiple Eye 1 missions involving numerous hurricanes, we will generate even better weather models and more accurate predictions. We may not be able to stop global warming, but we can get a better handle on adapting to it through the groundbreaking work of Eye 1."

Our next stop was the engine room housing the cutting-edge nuclear supercavitation engine that would propel us at unheard of speeds through the ocean. This powerful engine was linked to the boat's supercomputers which constantly made fine adjustments to the engine's performance characteristics enabling the engine to perform optimally in all ocean conditions.

Rubbing his hands over the smooth housing of the engine, Sean chirped, "She's my baby and I will keep her in tip-top shape. I know each nut and bolt in this thing and have come up with maintenance protocols that cover every possible scenario of engine malfunctions. With the aid of the supercomputers I will be able to view all engine working parts in real time with 3D video streaming. Nothing will get by me."

Moving back to the crew area of the boat, everyone was anxious to take a look at their completed cabins. All cabins were a standard size with the same amenities so that no crewmember was singled out to be more important than other crewmembers.

"There are no class distinctions on this boat, as elitism can be the scourge of crew camaraderie and effectiveness," I said. "No one will be consigned to a hammock above the bilge, only coming topside to swab the deck."

The cabin interiors were very plush with large comfortable Sleep Number beds, roomy bathrooms with bathtubs and showers, and huge 3D LED monitors that were connected to the ship's computer modules with complete network access to all ship's data and functions. A battery of microsized high-definition webcams located around the ship's working areas kept everyone informed of shipboard operations. Also, other sensors located throughout the outside of the hull continually monitored ocean conditions and relayed photos and data to the computer.

Looking at their separate cabins, Hatch and Angela expressed their unhappiness with this housing situation. "We need to collaborate constantly on our missions and want to be in the same cabin," Angela burst out. For his part, Hatch affirmed Angela's sentiments saying, "We need to be in close proximity if we are going to stay on top of things."

"No one else has their significant other here," I chimed in. "We can't single you guys out for special treatment while others need to go online for their erotic stimulation. Shipboard stress reduction requires all available outlets short of spooning. When we get into port, doing the wild thing will be an option for everybody."

CHAPTER FIFTEEN
IF IT RANES, IT POURS

My phone beeped and I looked at the new text message. The director of the National Weather Service was coming aboard and wanted to meet us in the command center. All of us barely fit in the elevator to take us to the top deck. Installing stairs in Eye 1 would have taken up too much space. For emergency purposes should the elevator fail, we installed a ladder-equipped tube that connected the top and bottom decks.

Rane McCloud was a distinguished-looking man in his early 60s, with a mane of white hair adorning his large Roman noble head. His authoritative manner commanded respect, suggesting he was an important person in his domain. Everyone shook hands with Mr. McCloud and welcomed him for his first visit to Eye 1.

"Thanks for inviting me here," McCloud said. "I couldn't wait to get a firsthand look at this new gizmo everyone is talking about. I can't believe the performance characteristics of this new boat, 100 mph+ underwater speed, dives to the deepest parts of the world's oceans, way beyond state-of-the-art in its weather information and data-gathering capabilities, not to mention it will be a hell of a lot of fun to be a crewmember. Can I come with you?"

"Well, we would like to have you aboard for our maiden mission," I said. "But I think you have some pretty big responsibilities back on terra firma. Perhaps you could be a crewmember after we have shaken the bugs out of her and she is purring like a kitten."

"That would be wonderful," McCloud replied. "And I should inform you now that I make a mean spaghetti and meatballs and an incomparable beef stew."

"Well," I said, "I am particularly partial to beef stew which is my own specialty. Perhaps we can have a cooking showdown like they do on those corny cooking shows where they make cooking look like a third world war. I think showbiz took a wrong turn when they tried to turn poached eggs into grenades. Hell, all cooking involves is mixing things up in different ways and deciding which way you are going to heat it up and for how long. If cooking was rocket science, pretty much everyone wouldn't know how to do it and there would be a lot more starving people on the planet."

"You've got something there," replied McCloud. "When are you going to show me how this baby works?"

Sean jumped in and said he would show Rane the engine and propulsion systems. Angela volunteered to explain the weather data-gathering technology onboard, Hack said he would showboat the supercomputers and software, and Hatch said he would expound on the captain's duties. For my part, as coordinator of the vessel's missions, I would describe to Rane how I hoped to tie everything together into one coherent purpose-driven unit.

The crewmembers showed Mr. McCloud around for several hours before he came into my quarters and thanked me for the tour. "I wish you god speed on your venture and mankind will be thanking you for your efforts," he said. "Likewise," I said.

Chapter Sixteen
TV Land

Next on the agenda was a meeting with R.E. Allity, whom everyone called R.E. for short, the joke being that R.E. meant *real enthusiastic*. R.E. had brought along several members of his production staff who wanted to scout placement of cameras in various locations around the interior of the vessel.

I shook hands with R.E. and told his staff they had free reign on Eye 1.

"How many production staff members do you think you will need onboard for *Eye of the Hurricane 1: The Reality Show*? I asked R.E. He replied, "I'm not exactly sure yet as we want to be as unobtrusive as possible to avoid gumming up your missions with TV production activity. The key to meeting that requirement is utilizing remotely operated cameras to capture the action with no production staff in the way of the crew."

"That sounds good," I responded. "We don't

have one professional actor in the crew, so you will be filming live action in real time. Our primary concern is that the final edited one-hour episodes could compromise our missions and malign the integrity of our organization."

"You don't have to worry about that," R.E. said. "We will run the final edited film by you and the Eye 1 board to make sure your content concerns are properly addressed and dealt with. Given we are part of the Eye 1 organization and support its mission statement, it is not in our interest to over-sensationalize and hype up the show to the detriment of Eye 1."

"By the same token," R.E. continued, "the shows have to be entertaining and interesting enough to hold TV watchers' attention. This will be a real life version of the sixties TV series, *Voyage to the Bottom of the Sea*, and will confirm that truth is always stranger than fiction."

Chapter Seventeen
Trash Talking

I sat with Hatch in our living room, both of us glued to the Weather Channel which was covering the first hurricane of the season, Hurricane Emily. Currently at Category 1 status, Hurricane Emily was headed directly for Cuba after striking glancing blows at Puerto Rico and the Dominican Republic, causing minor damage and no fatalities.

Hatch was drinking Jack Daniels and I had a Sam Adams lager in my hand, both of us snacking on a big bowl of heavily buttered popcorn with lots of salt on it.

"It will pick up speed and intensity after it leaves Cuba and hits the warm waters of the Gulf of Mexico," Hatch mumbled while stuffing a huge wad of popcorn into his mouth. "If Eye 1 was following this hurricane, we would want to intercept it when it reaches Gulf waters. However, given the speed capabilities of Eye 1, we could catch it before it leaves

Cuba, giving us a head start in building a full data set of the storm.

"Roger," I said, "we should intercept hurricanes as soon as we can which means making well-educated guesses about the path and intensity of developing storms. I am working with the United States Air Force to see if we can use their largest transport plane, the C5-M Super Galaxy, to quickly move Eye 1 to the general area where hurricanes are forming. Once Eye 1 is in service it will be stationed in southern Florida and can probably reach many developing hurricanes before they get big, but we have to cover ourselves in the event a worst-case scenario occurs and we have to deploy on short notice a great distance from our base."

Hatch and I went for a run before resuming our posts in front of the TV. Hurricane Emily had been upgraded to Category 3 status as it proceeded across the warm Gulf of Mexico waters, with landfall expected in southern Alabama near Mobile in two days. The doorbell rang and Angela came in to review the situation with us and give her current analysis of Emily.

"Hey sweetheart," Hatch chortled as he stuffed his mouth with more popcorn and took a good swig of Jack Daniels. "How about I get you a Tequila Sunrise and a big bowl of popcorn?"

"That is fine," Angela replied, "but no butter or

salt on the popcorn, that stuff is death for you guys."

"Do you guys want a demonstration of the computer Hack custom-built for me?" Angela continued.

"Of course," I said, "but where is it? I don't see any computer on or near you. I think you are pulling a fast one on us."

Conceived and built by Hack, Angela's new computer was light-years ahead of current laptop and desktop technology, providing her direct easy access to the gargantuan computing power of our shipboard supercomputers and land-based supercomputers at Eye 1 headquarters and National Weather Services offices nationwide. Angela's computer connected to the supercomputers via a *cloud* specially designed for Eye 1.

Angela walked in front of us and then turned to face us. Immediately, a 3D holographic image appeared about three feet in front of her, like a typical computer desktop screen, but completely devoid of content, a blank slate.

"You are fooling with us, Angie, this is a good parlor trick but nothing more," said Hatch. "Come off it."

Seconds later the Google search engine appeared in thin air with the name "Hatch Moniker" typed in the search box.

"Hatch, what would you like to know about

yourself?" Angela said, as a list of Hatch references appeared on the screen. "Let's take a look at it, guys, and there better be no other women out there."

The holographic image scrolled down the list containing considerable information we already knew about Hatch with one item causing us to gasp quickly and stare at Hatch.

The blurb said: *"Hatch Moniker arrested for indecent exposure while appearing naked in the Fourth of July parade. Mr. Moniker, a decorated Navy Seal, was charged for indecent exposure after he ran naked across the parade route between the Fundamental Baptist Float and Playboy Magazine's float. When asked why he did it, Moniker replied, 'I was off duty'."*

We both immediately chastised Hatch then started laughing in uncontrollable fits of mirth that ended with us rolling around the floor in front of him.

Nonplussed as always, Hatch responded, "Don't you remember streaking in the early 70s? Everybody was doing it then."

"I remember streaking but I don't think young Angela is familiar with this fad," I said. "Not quite everybody was streaking back then."

"Okay, Angela," I said. "Where is the device?"

Angela touched the front of her pink blouse and said, "This is it. The computer is built into my top and the holographic image is projected out through a button. I communicate with the computer directly from a neural net-connected microprocessor in my skull, which enables my thoughts to be transmitted to my limbs and other bodily functions. This technology is an offshoot of Segway inventor Dean Kamen's brain-controlled artificial hand."

"I want one too," Hatch said, "on my Navy Seal sweatshirt."

"Everyone on the crew will be getting one of these devices before we launch," I said. "And they will be built into the Eye 1 uniforms I am designing now. If General George Patton could design a new tank corps uniform, I want to design our clothing."

Patton designed a new tank corps uniform in the 1930s which was not accepted by the army. Topped off with a green football helmet, Patton's uniform earned him the nickname "The Green Hornet."

Chapter Eighteen
Trial

Our day of reckoning was fast approaching as Eye 1 prepared to go to sea on our first mission. The only serious hurricane of the season thus far, Hurricane Emily, had fizzled into a tropical storm before it made landfall in Alabama.

The boat was nearly ready for sea trials scheduled to begin next week. The crew was honed to a fine razor's edge and excited to be finally getting off the starting block.

R.E. had set up all the cameras in the vessel and was ready to go with production of *Eye 1: The Reality Show*. He already had film in the can of all aspects of design and preparation of Eye 1, including crew training and clips describing the new technologies that would set Eye 1 apart from any vessel currently operating in the world's oceans.

Rane McCloud was chomping at the bit to get the first Eye 1 data for the National Weather Service to examine and study. Rane called me and said he had improved his spaghetti and meatball and stew recipes so that he would kick my ass in our televised cook-off aboard ship when he was able to crew with us on a future mission.

The Eye 1 board and major investors were impressed on their recent tour of the vessel confirming their cash had been properly utilized by the working group of architects, designers, engineers, and workers actually building the submarine. Mr. Soffit had commented, "I wish I had one of these to play with in my bathtub when I was a kid. I didn't get a train set until I purchased the Burlington Northern Santa Fe Railroad a couple of years ago."

I planned a ship christening ceremony late the following week to celebrate Eye 1's move from dry dock via marine airbags to the ocean. These airbags deflate creating a downward slope from the launching vessel to the ocean. A special bottle of drinkable 200-year-old champagne recovered from a Baltic shipwreck was going to be broken on the bow of Eye 1 by the Finnish diver and pub owner who found the wreck. Sean had come up with a method of saving the wine after the bottle was broken so that all present at the ceremony could have a taste of the unique effervescent liquid. We all hoped Eye 1 would be as strong and durable as the ancient wine bottle.

In charge of the christening ceremony, my wife

Honeybunch was in a frenzy working out final details of the affair. She had gotten together all crew families to help with Eye 1's christening and lined up Shannon to do a special blessing of the sub attended by her husband R.E. and all major sponsors of the Eye 1 project.

CHAPTER NINETEEN
ALL ABOARD

The christening ceremony went well and the crew was anxious to finally get out to sea on Eye 1. On the morning of our departure all crewmembers met in the command center to review and check our systems and procedures before our shakedown cruise. Everything was a go and we could only hope we had covered all the bases in preparation for this moment.

Hatch was in his glory when he moved the joystick to make way at 10 mph as we eased away from port into the open ocean. Eye 1 moved smoothly and quietly along the surface as Hack and Sean monitored LED screens replete with all the data coming from engine and computer systems. Hatch was particularly concerned that our sonar and radar systems were picking up any other boat traffic in the area, so that we could steer clear of these obstacles.

Angela was carefully monitoring weather

forecasts that could negatively affect our trial cruise. Doc Ozz was busy checking crewmembers' vital signs relayed from sensors on their bodies to his Apple Watch and the supercomputers. In case of a power outage onboard ship, Ozz's Apple Watch was lithium-ion battery powered as were the body sensors, so that Ozz could stay on top of medical issues on the vessel even if the lights went out. In addition, special lithium ion battery banks donated by Elon Musk, owner of Tesla Motors, would provide emergency power if the nuclear engine went down. These reserve power supplies would keep our life support systems working and enable us to limp back to port if disaster struck.

After a discussion with Sean and Hack about vessel performance characteristics, all in the normal range, Hatch beefed up the vessel speed to 30 mph and readied the boat for its first dive below the surface. Simply by moving the joystick, Hatch initiated our first dive. As we all looked at the simulated front window, sunlight was replaced by bubbles and darkness as we dipped below the ocean. Leveling off at 300 feet everyone cheered as we glided through the water almost effortlessly, a very low hum the only indication that a powered vessel was advancing through the ocean.

I declared lunchtime and crewmembers took turns rotating through the kitchen area while the remainder of the crew stood watch in the command center. When I took my turn for lunch, I heated up a frozen hamburger in the microwave and started eating it when Hatch came in the kitchen.

"You know that nuked food tastes like hell," Hatch commented, before throwing a big ribeye steak into the frying pan and cutting up some onions and potatoes which were soon sizzling alongside the meat.

"To each his own," I admonished Hatch before leaving the kitchen to return to my duties in the command center. The supercomputers were recording a complete log of all ship's functions and performance characteristics, analyzed minute by minute by Sean and Hack onboard, and Eye 1's headquarters staff back in Florida. More importantly, a variety of types of proprietary software designed exclusively by Hack and his land-bound associates, were studying Eye 1's performance data at warp speed to give us an immediate heads-up if any untoward anomalies occurred.

"I'm pretty confident in the software," Hack said, "but I expect to be writing more code to fine tune things as we move through our cruise." Hack's genius level ability to create software and modify it on the fly, likened to master guitarist Jose Feliciano's ability to tune his guitar as he performed live, with the pure sound not giving away Jose's string tension adjustments.

Back in the command center, everything ran smoothly as we maintained our speed, depth, and course. When Hatch got back from lunch, he said that we were ready to dive deeper and take her up to full speed, approximately 127 mph.

This was going to be the moment of truth that we had all been waiting for, the first test of whether Eye 1 would fulfill its design specifications and carve a special niche in nautical history. Hatch ordered everyone to strap themselves into their seats and brace for the dramatic acceleration we were soon going to experience.

Hatch pushed the joystick steadily forward and tremendous gravitational forces slammed us back into our seats. We gasped for breath, as Eye 1 catapulted ahead at 1500 feet depth, charting a course for the open ocean. The window was completely dark except for the occasional spot of light flickering for a millisecond as tiny organisms in the water projected their luminescence. As we surged past 60 mph the LED readouts were changing numbers faster than a slot machine in Las Vegas. Beads of sweat formed on Hatch's forehead as he checked the instruments to make sure the gas bubble was forming properly around Eye 1.

It was the gas bubble that made it possible for us to achieve these spellbinding speeds as we plowed through the water. Our ride steadied as the gas bubble formed completely and our speed swept past 80 mph. We were in unknown territory now as our boat rocketed forward at speeds only dreamt about by early submariners. Attaining our maximum speed of 127 mph, we were cruising at 10 times the speed of World War 1 submarines.

We needed to maintain this speed for two hours to prove that Eye 1 could operate at full throttle for extended periods. Most of the time our missions would not require maximum speed, but when we were chasing hurricanes to get in the center of the eye, the sooner we got there the more data we could collect.

Everyone slowly relaxed as Eye 1 moved at top speed under the ocean. Angela got up from her weather station and came over to wipe the sweat off Hatch's forehead, before it dripped on his instrument panels.

"You are holding up well, honey," said Angela. "Maybe I can give you a neck massage later to lower your stress level."

"That would be fine," Hatch replied.

Doc Ozz chimed in saying, "What about massages for the rest of us? We need them too."

"Well, you guys can get in line after Hatch," Angela replied. "I'm not going to run a massage parlor on this ship. I have too much work to do.

Surely there is someone else who can give massages."

"But we don't want a massage from another *guy*," Ozz said.

Angela returned to her station to check the latest weather data in the area we were headed for. At the end of our two-hour full speed test, we were going to turn south for San Juan, Puerto Rico, to briefly dock for a full inspection of the boat.

The crew was suddenly jolted alert as if in an airplane encountering heavy turbulence. But 1500 feet under the ocean, the sensation was more like rolling on a trampoline with other people jumping up and down at the same time. Luckily, the special computer-controlled suspension system on our crew seats minimized body movement or we would have been thrown around the cabin like rag dolls.

Hatch quickly reduced speed to 75 mph and the turbulence effect immediately ceased. Sean and Hack reviewed their control panels and data systems to try and figure out what had caused the shaking of Eye 1, as we couldn't have hit an object in the water or the vessel would have been severely damaged if not destroyed.

Hatch cut speed back to 20 mph allowing a thorough examination of the crisis to be conducted with the assistance of all hands. Everyone spread out through the sub to visually inspect for any damage while our supercomputers did diagnostics of all shipboard systems. We wanted to get to the bottom of this problem fast or it could jeopardize the ability of Eye 1 to successfully carry out her missions.

Arriving back at the command center, all crewmembers reported they had not seen damage anywhere on the sub. Sean and Hack quickly conferred on the results of the diagnostic which hadn't yet identified the cause of the problem. Sean asked Hack to run the performance data through multiple software programs in order to isolate the specific source of the error.

Moments later Hack's screen came alive with words describing the cause of the problem. "A malfunction occurred in the software interface connecting the ship's electrostatically controlled gyroscope and the supercavitation drive. This interface must be modified to eliminate the motion error."

With the assistance of Sean, Hack quickly got to work writing new code for the software interface. Ten minutes later Hack jumped up from his seat excited about the code solution he found for this problem.

"I think I've got it," exhorted Hack. "There was a small error in the code which caused the gyroscope malfunction and I think I have corrected it. I will program a few more simulations to make sure I'm right before we run her up to full speed again."

Our onboard reality show producer, Jeff Huston,

came above to the command center with his two assistants to find out what happened. "Not to worry, Jeff," I said. "I think we have a handle on the problem. Very soon we will be running Eye 1 up to full speed again and hopefully won't have a repeat of this incident."

"That's good," Jeff replied. "The turbulence threw our equipment for a loop and we are getting everything stabilized again."

Jeff and Hatch were not getting along very well, Hatch concerned about the TV crew impeding crew operations.

Looking directly at Jeff, Hatch told him, "Can't you guys lay low more so you don't get in our way so much? This is really pissing me off."

"We are doing our best," Jeff replied. "But it won't be much of a show if we can't freely move around the ship. We need to see you guys in action so we can get a real feel for what is going on."

Hatch sneered and said, "Too bad we can't attach you guys to the outside of the window so you can look in and watch us."

Hack gave the "all clear" indicating that systems were ready for another test at full speed. Hatch pushed the joystick forward slowly as we were pushed back in our seats by the acceleration. Diving to 3,000 feet we felt no change in pressure in the cabin and no nuts or bolts were popping on the inside of

Eye 1's hull.

We were now at approximately three times the depth limits of conventional nuclear submarines, a mere fraction of our planned depth capabilities of 38,000 feet where the deepest parts of the ocean lie. Eye 1 could explore all depths of the ocean instead of only shallow surface waters accessible by US Navy nuclear subs.

In terms of construction, Eye 1 was light years ahead of early submarines held together by bailing wire and iron hoops. Eye 1 incorporated technology that will be built into Virginia Class Block V submarines within the next decade. This advanced technology included modular isolated decks, open system architecture, and technology insert bundles that allow future modular technology to be incorporated into Eye 1.

Hull design was also taken to the next level with integrated tube and hull forging, a process involving welding parts of the boat together making it possible to manufacture key parts of the submarine before final integration of the boat. Built into the inside of the titanium hull, Jim Cameron's syntactic foam reinforced the entire superstructure of the boat.

As we accelerated past 80 mph the ride was still smooth with no turbulence. When we got to 127 mph, our top speed, we anxiously awaited another disaster that didn't come. Eye 1 performed flawlessly for the next two hours and we were able to carry out our regular duties. Slowing down to 40 mph we expected to cruise into port at Puerto Rico sometime the next morning.

Tired from the stress and stimulation of our first day on the boat, the crew retired to their cabins with Sean and Hack taking the first four-hour watch, with Hatch and I scheduled for the second watch. Until all crewmembers were trained so they could supervise watches, we wanted to keep either Hatch or Sean in charge. Of course, our supercomputers were on watch all the time, but there was not yet a replacement for human hands and eyes at the helm to assist all the gee-whiz technology.

Hatch and I were the last crewmembers to settle down in the kitchen to make our evening meals. I volunteered to make a fine beef stew that Hatch and I could share. I made the stew and put it on simmer for a while, before brewing a pot of coffee for the two of us. Hatch and I wanted to compare notes about the shakedown cruise so far, for the purpose of tweaking our operations to work more smoothly.

"I'm fairly pleased with things so far," I told Hatch, as I stirred the stew and put some more beef oxo cubes in it. "But I'm not happy with the friction between you and Jeff. The reality show team has a difficult job to do in this setting."

"But we are the bread and butter of this

111

operation," Hatch replied. "The reality show is only window dressing."

"I totally disagree," I said. "If we don't get our message out about what we are doing for the planet, our effectiveness is diminished exponentially. We can't throw the baby out with the bathwater. Plus, the show will likely generate considerable revenue for the Eye 1 program. Please have more patience with these TV guys."

"Okay, I get your point," Hatch conceded. "I will talk to Jeff tomorrow and see what we can work out."

I filled a bowl of stew for each of us and poured two cups of coffee, then sliced up a loaf of fresh hot bread Hatch had made. Hatch devoured the stew and quickly filled his bowl with another big helping of the age-old dish.

"Good stuff, Plug," Hatch said. "Too bad we can't wash it down with a bottle of my mountain flower wine. By the way, I want in on that cook-off between you and McCloud. My bread will blow you guys out of the water."

"Once we've completed this cruise, Honeybunch and I will make a big batch of stew at home and you can supply the wine and bread," I replied.

CHAPTER TWENTY
PORT

Early the next morning Eye 1 surfaced just outside the port of San Juan and we all met on the observation deck to watch our entry into the harbor.

There was no fanfare as we moved toward the dock, the exact identity of our boat not known to anyone in Puerto Rico. We were classified as a US Navy vessel for security purposes, so that terrorists or other belligerent parties would have less opportunity to damage or destroy Eye 1 while we were in port.

I shouted, "*Ahoy maties*" to the Navy dock crew as we eased into the moorings and made our lines fast. An automated gangway unfurled across the passage from the boat to the pier, and as soon as we got the all clear from the dockworkers, we made our way to the dock. On hand to greet us were Eye 1 headquarters staff flown in from Florida to discuss the results of our test mission so far.

"We have rooms for you guys booked at the

Marriott," Gob Tween said. "Climb into the van." Gob was our "fixer," charged with arranging details of our shore visits and generally keeping us happy as we attended to mission tasks.

Arriving at the hotel, crewmembers settled into their rooms before coming to my room for a meeting.

Everyone was in chairs or sitting on the bed, anxiously awaiting my comments. "I have an important announcement to make. I assume all of you have been following the story of the missing Malaysian Airliner, Flight MH370. Two days ago, pings were heard which matched black boxes on the missing airliner in a search area in the Southern Ocean about 1200 miles off the coast of Perth, Australia. As you know, the pings are emitted for a period of about thirty days before the black box batteries run out. Search officials think they have about two weeks to find the black boxes."

"We have been asked by the White House to assist in the search as part of our trial cruise," I said. "Our unique capabilities may be a big help in finding the crashed plane. How do you feel about doing this?"

A chorus of yeas greeted my remarks, the crew affirming Eye 1's commitment to look for the missing plane.

"We will have to complete our boat inspection ASAP and stock up with plenty of food and other supplies," I continued. "Hatch, I want you to check in with search officials as to what their needs are and how Eye 1 can best dovetail with their operations. Hack will assist you in this task and make sure our computer systems are set up with the best software for finding the plane. Angela, I want you to get a handle on the weather down there and determine how it will affect our search efforts. Doc Ozz will make sure our medical kit is ready and everyone is checked out for fitness."

"How are we going to get there on time to help with the search, Perth, Australia is 11,500 miles from here?" asked Doc Ozz.

"Well, Doc, a USAF C-5M Super Galaxy transport plane arriving at San Juan Airport tomorrow will be specially outfitted to handle Eye 1 which will be trucked in a convoy over to San Juan airport," I said. "We will all ride on the Super Galaxy with Eye 1, and will refuel midair two times before landing in Perth."

Intensive preparations began as we readied ourselves for our first real mission. We would have liked to have more time to test Eye 1 and iron out her bugs, but we could make a real difference in the search for the missing plane, which had already covered a number of areas in the South China Sea and the Indian Ocean, based upon sketchy data received from MH370. Amazingly, if a basic $200 transmitting GPS had been purchased at Radio Shack and carried on the plane, we would probably have known the exact location of the crash site by now.

Assuming that responsible people know what they are doing can be a grave error. Airplane manufacturers and airline officials get entrenched in their narrow bureaucratic tunnel vision and are afraid to stick their necks out like mindless functionaries everywhere. Always trying to cut costs in the super competitive airline industry, airlines seemingly couldn't cough up $200 for a readily available consumer product. Dumb, dumb, and dumber.

Assisting operations to load Eye 1 into the giant transport plane, I was amazed that engineers could figure out a way to bring our boat to the airport and load it up on the largest cargo capacity military transport plane in the world. Viewing Eye 1 sitting behind the C-5A Super Galaxy on the runway, the problem was akin to figuring out how they get the caramel in a Caramilk bar. Aiding the process was the special kneeling landing gear on the aircraft that made it easier to move a heavy load from the tarmac into the plane.

Loadmasters performed a variety of calculations to determine the exact position Eye 1 would ride in the cargo hold, so that its weight would be evenly distributed over the plane's center of gravity. Then Eye 1 was slowly winched and pushed up into the large cargo compartment, and locks and rails were set in place by the loadmasters to prevent shifting of the load. Eye 1's crew and the loadmasters would ride in the rear cargo flight deck facing the back of the plane.

We finished our breakfasts at the airport cafe before heading out to board the plane. Only forty-eight hours had passed between my announcement until our takeoff scheduled in one hour.

Settled in our seats we chatted with the loadmasters about the challenges they faced in getting Eye 1 on their plane.

"How did you guys manage it?" Sean asked. "I'll bet you have never carried any cargo similar to Eye 1."

"No, we haven't, and I'm not looking forward to doing it again," Chief Loadmaster Steve Addor said. "The biggest problem we had was squeezing Eye 1 into our cargo hold, and quite a few adjustments were made to gain the extra space to fit Eye 1."

"When do we get a ride in Eye 1?" asked Steve.

"After you get us to Perth, we will answer that question," Sean replied with a smile on his face.

CHAPTER TWENTY-ONE
SEARCH

The sound was deafening as we lifted off from San Juan on our way to Perth.

The flight was uneventful, with Doc Ozz and myself playing cribbage while the rest of the crew watched movies or listened to music. Hatch managed to scratch up a giant bowl of heavily salted and buttered popcorn which he and the other men dug into. Angela gave them a dirty look as she ate her granola bar.

"You guys should be ashamed of yourselves," Angela said. "I thought I had straightened you out on popcorn. I am going to have to put you guys on an intravenous vitamin solution while you are sleeping."

"Are you sure you want to do that?" Hatch replied. "That would be a little kinky to say the least. I'd rather you tie me up."

It was exciting for everyone to watch the two

118

midair refuelings, as the tanker plane eased up so close to our transport we could almost touch it. Then a hose snaked out of the tanker, somehow making the connection with the intake port of our fuel tanks, quickly topping off our fuel and saving us several hours flight time by not having to land and refuel.

Touching down in Perth, we were all tired from the long flight but eager to get to work searching for the missing plane.

After Eye 1 was moved from the plane and docked in Perth Harbor, we awaited a visit from Koala Dundee, the Australian former defense chief coordinating the MH370 search in the Southern Ocean.

Mr. Dundee arrived in the command center, just as we were completing final checklists for our search mission.

"Hey mates, thanks for dropping in and helping us with the search," Dundee said. "We are running out of time to locate those black boxes. The pings from the boxes will end soon. We have pulled out all the stops but still no luck."

"Based on your review of the situation, what advice can you give us for the best way to integrate Eye 1 into our search?" Dundee continued.

"First, we would like access to the recordings of those beep signals you received," I said. "The next time these signals are transmitted they can be picked up by our sonar and other special radar and listening equipment."

"Also, we want a liaison from your office to come onboard and stay in constant communication with you, updating you on our progress in the search."

"That is a good idea," Koala replied. "The Bluefin 21 side scan sonar submersible robot towed behind the Ocean Shield has reached her depth limit of 14,800 feet."

Bluefin 21 was the device that picked up some of the pinger beeps, along with pinger signals received by the Chinese ship, *Haixun 01*. The deepest point in the search area was 24,000 feet, well within the capabilities of Eye 1.

Search planes from Australia, China, United States, Great Britain, Japan, New Zealand, and other countries had combed the surface of the ocean for crash debris, but only found fishing debris and other waste items not connected with the loss of MH370.

"We need you to get to the bottom and move around for a while, so we locate those pings," Dundee continued. "With Eye 1's speed, you will be able cover a large area fast and map the bottom as you go. As you know, the vast majority of the sea floor is unmapped by sonar. Currently, most ocean bottom data comes from satellite radar and/or gravity measurements. We know more about Mars than the bottom of the oceans."

"Yeah, if we had a fleet of Eye 1's, we could map the bottom of all the oceans in a reasonable time frame," Hatch said.

"Maybe that will happen sometime," replied Dundee.

Completing his tour of Eye 1, including discussions with all Eye 1 crewmembers and a look-see at all of our equipment and technology, Koala expressed his confidence in our contribution to the search effort and thanked us for coming this far to help.

As Dundee walked on the ramp and headed for the dock, I shouted out to him, "And if you are a good cook you can take part in our televised cook-off with me and Rane McCloud and Hatch."

"Shrimp on the barbie is my thing, it will knock your socks off," was Dundee's parting comment.

Soon we were making our way out of Perth Harbor and heading toward the search area 1200 miles southwest of Perth.

Hatch dived to 500 feet and then cranked Eye 1 up to full speed, with our projected arrival at the search area in under twelve hours. Search headquarters had e-mailed us the recorded ping information and Hack was analyzing it with software on the supercomputers.

"I think I have a pretty good handle where these pings are from," Hack said. "We can cruise over that area and see what we get."

"The weather is really bad out there, with forty foot waves and a 60 mph wind. I hope we don't have to surface at any time," Angela said. "By the way, did anyone have a good time in Perth, other than Hatch?"

The air quickly came out of Hatch's sails, and he averted his eyes from Angela's penetrating gaze.

Hack chirped in, "What about that, Hatch, what happened in Perth?"

"What happened in Perth stays in Perth," Hatch replied, an angry tone in his voice.

"Yes, Hatch, what about that fight you had with that owner of a cattle station?" Angela asked.

"I only put him in a headlock, I didn't hurt him. When I am insulted like that I have to take action," was Hatch's rejoinder.

"Tell the truth, Hatch, you were coming on to his wife," Angela said.

"No, I got fed up with him calling her just another Sheila. I told her that Sheila is a fine name and she didn't need this kind of bullshit from her asshole husband," Hatch said. "He called me a wanker and it was on."

"Don't you know, Hatch, that women are called Sheilas here?" Angela continued. "And wanker is a general term of disparagement, not a one-handed backslap about your teenage sex life."

"Well, I don't know anything about Australia

except that bathtubs here drain the opposite way from our bathtubs," Hatch said. "I couldn't figure it out at first, but the maid told me when she came to clean our room."

I told everyone to "get some food and sleep before we arrive at our search area. Then we will need all hands on deck."

I decided to call my wife and find out what was going on back home. Honeybunch answered the phone on the first ring and I said, "Hi Hon," before updating her on activities on Eye 1 and she telling me what was going on back home.

"You are getting a lot of calls dear," Honeybunch said. "I think word has leaked out about what you guys are doing down there."

"That's just great," I said. "Now, all eyes will be on us and we will have to deliver, no matter what the situation is."

I had trouble getting to sleep that night, worried about what the next day would bring in our efforts to find the missing plane. I thought about the people on that plane and what they had been through as the Boeing 777 tumbled out of control into the ocean. Did they all die on impact? Did some of them survive as the plane dipped under the surface and gradually settled to the bottom of the ocean? Were there air pockets in the cabin of the plane that enabled some of them to breathe for a while as the plane sunk deeper?

I speculated on all the theories of why the plane abruptly went off course in the opposite direction of Peking where it was to land. Was the flight hijacked by terrorists? Were the pilots somehow involved in the disappearance of the plane, diverting it somewhere for personal gain, or did they commit suicide? Did the plane land somewhere on terra firma for some nefarious purpose? Were the passengers being held captive for some future ransom attempt? Was it a cyber hijacking via the plane's flight control system?

All these possibilities tumbled around in my head as I tried to imagine what happened to MH370. Until the loss of MH370, Amelia Earhart's disappearance in the South Pacific in 1937 was the greatest mystery in the history of aviation. In 1991, a piece of aluminum belonging to Earhart's twin-engine Lockheed Electra was found on the tiny, uninhabited island of Nikumaroro, between Hawaii and Australia.

Researchers determined the aluminum sheet was a patch of metal installed on the Electra during the aviatrix's eight-day stay in Miami, which was the fourth stop on her attempt to circumnavigate the globe. Earhart made a forced landing on Nikumaroro's smooth, flat coral reef. Earhart and her navigator became castaways and eventually died on the atoll, which is some 350 miles southeast of Howland Island where Earhart was scheduled to stop for refueling. The International Group for

Historic Aircraft Recovery analyzed the patch and determined it was a part of Earhart's plane.

"The Miami Patch was an expedient field repair," a TIGHAR spokesman told a reporter. "Its complex fingerprint of dimensions, proportions, materials, and rivet patterns was as unique to Earhart's Electra as a fingerprint is to an individual."

Was it going to take six decades to find a clue to the disappearance of MH370? Did we have the technology and investigative expertise in the early 21st century to solve this mystery?

I awoke as we closed in on the search area. The crew assembled in the command center for a final briefing prior to commencement of our search. Everyone was excited but subdued as I started to speak.

"This is it, guys," I said. "This is where the rubber meets the road as we, pardon the pun, get to the bottom of this mystery. We must leave no stone unturned or any unnatural sounds left unexplained. Think of the families of the missing passengers when you are doing your work. Are there any questions?"

"Do you think we have gotten all the necessary information from the Malaysian government about what they know about this incident?" Hack asked. "The Malaysians seem to be incompetent in conducting an investigation of this magnitude. They are divulging information in dribs and drabs and their data often conflicts with itself, shedding doubt on the veracity of their press releases."

"We have to work with what we have," I responded. "But a high degree of skepticism about any existing data or theories is a very good idea. We have to roll everything over in our own minds before committing to any particular action plan."

Hatch initiated a steep dive while Hack turned on all our sonar, sensor, and camera equipment for mapping and analyzing the ocean floor. Strapped tightly in our seats, we rocketed downward toward the bottom, finally leveling off about 500 feet above the ocean floor at a depth of 12,675 feet. The feeling was eerie this far below the ocean surface, almost as if we had entered a different world.

With all our lights on we could barely make out the bottom looking through our front window screen. Jagged cliffs and deep ravines that could swallow up any craft including a large jet, crisscrossed the ocean floor, with an astounding variety of sea creatures surviving at this depth. Fishes, corals, crustaceans, jellyfishes, and worms—all have adapted to life in this challenging environment where no plant life exists.

Many of these animals look quite alien to us. Some have huge eyes, or eyes on long stalks that capture the little existing light. Others seem to be all mouth. Their gaping jaws filled with fang-like teeth are always open, ready to capture whatever morsels fall from above, these food tidbits known as "marine snow" to biologists. Still other deep-sea animals have transparent bodies you can see through, enabling them to blend right in with the water.

As we glided along the bottom at 60 mph, capturing and recording a variety of information with our numerous sensors, the crew was spellbound with this history-making first deep-sea voyage on Eye 1. We were charting new waters, going where no ocean vessel had been before, while conducting an important mission for humanity.

Hack jumped up from his chair shouting, "I've got a ping, I've got a ping!" Hatch immediately slowed Eye 1 down to 20 mph and began circling the location of the ping. Hack put the ping sounds on the command center speakers and we could hear the sound's one-ping-a-second cadence, matching that of equipment known to be on the plane. Hack ran the ping sounds through the software containing the pings picked up earlier by the Bluefish 21 and the Chinese ship, also comparing them with the sound pattern designed into the MH370's two black boxes.

All three sounds matched, except that the Bluefish 21 pings and the Chinese intercepted pings were at a slightly lower frequency than the MH370 black box recorder standard sounds. Optimism increased based on the fact the pings were detected near an arc where an Inmarsat satellite had last communicated with the plane.

Caution stemmed from the ping's 33.3 kHz frequency, slightly lower than the black box's 37.5 kHz design frequency. There were also concerns because the two ping detection sites were miles apart. Experts said crash damage or deep ocean pressures could alter the pinger frequency and the plane's two black boxes could have been separated during an explosion or crash, and noted that sounds can travel far, and even echo, in underwater environments.

As we closed in on the source of the ping, it became louder and louder until we could see the so-called black box via our external cameras. The recording boxes are generally not black in color, but usually bright orange, as they are intended to be spotted and recovered after incidents. We nudged Eye 1 closer and closer to the small orange box which was slightly wedged between two sharp rock projections.

Our custom-designed robot arm was manufactured by the same Canadian company that produced the Space Shuttle *Canadarm*. Frank Mee is credited as the inventor of the *Canadarm,* its design inspired by the opening and closing of a camera's iris. Mee's design won over claw-like mechanisms also under consideration. The *Canadarm* can move very accurately and slowly over a distance of millimeters and it can move with similar precision at higher speeds.

During more than fifty space shuttle missions and 7,000 orbits around the earth, the *Canadarm* never malfunctioned. Indeed, the arm was used to help solve other problems on the shuttle, everything from knocking ice off the fuselage of the orbiter to fixing the Hubble Space Telescope, to assembling the new international space station. The *Canadarm* is truly one of Canada's greatest engineering achievements and a major contribution to the United States space program.

We all watched in fascination as our multifunctional front window-video monitor displayed images from cameras on the *Canadarm* and Eye 1's hull. Operating the arm vehicle, which he had practiced many times, Hack smoothly moved the unit's complicated appendage toward the orange box, readily visible under the bright lights of Eye 1 and the arm. First nudging one of the rocks away from the box, Hack enclosed the box in the unique *Canadarm* iris replicating grapple, grasping the box very softly with minimal disturbance to the surface and contents of the container.

The arm gradually retracted into its smooth hull enclosure, thereby minimizing hydrodynamic drag associated with conventional deep-sea submersible apparatus that stuck out on all sides of a vessel, greatly inhibiting speed of movement and inviting more potential damage to the vehicle similar to the risk of sticking your arm out of an all-terrain vehicle while travelling through thick brush.

Groundbreaking in its conception and design, use of Eye 1's arm was the first time an external device of this type was deployed from the inside of a deep-sea parent vessel. Until Eye 1, robotic arms on small deep-sea submersibles were attached to the outside of the relatively tiny, slow-moving vessels including Jim Cameron's Deep-sea Challenger.

Also, Eye 1's arm was part of a remotely controlled platform not attached to Eye 1's hull, making it possible for the *Canadarm* to be moved around at will within a one-mile range of Eye 1, totally joystick controlled by Hack on the mother ship. Special sonar equipment and sensors aboard both the arm and Eye 1 enabled the free-ranging picker-upper to operate at the precise tolerances required by these delicate operations.

The arm vessel, dubbed *Hack's Grabber* by the crew, returned to Eye 1 and carefully aligned itself with its special deployment bay utilizing lasers on Eye 1 and the arm vehicle. Never before in submersible history had a remotely operated vehicle been deployed from a sub at this great depth. Regularly, United States Navy nuclear subs deploy ROVs, including vehicles piloted by Navy Seals for fast shore insertion, at shallow depths not affected by monumental pressures found in the deep ocean.

Eye 1's state-of-the-art deployment bay was enabled by new technology that compensated for the massive ocean pressures trying to squeeze Eye 1 into a flat plate of twisted metal. This new deep-sea hydraulic pressure compensation technology was advancing rapidly due to the emergence of oil, gas, and mining activities taking place on the deep ocean floor, heretofore untapped by mankind. As always, the lure of potential profits drove the development of new technologies.

Everyone wanted to look at the black box which was held in a pressurized container prior to being examined by the Federal Aviation Administration and other parties connected to the search effort. We were to hand the black box off to the Ocean Shield the next morning which would transport it by helicopter to Perth and then by jet back to Washington, DC.

"The box looks like it is in good shape," said Angela. "After what it went through in the crash, it is amazing it's still in one piece."

"Yeah, that box is built like a brick shithouse, it can take any kind of abuse," Hatch added.

Now that we had found one of the black boxes, our search efforts redoubled to find pieces of wreckage on the ocean floor. So far we only found some old fishing nets and one container that must have fallen off a freighter. We were not sure what was in it, if anything, but didn't have time to pry the container open and check inside.

We gradually widened our search circle, but still saw nothing resembling wreckage from the Boeing 777. I called a meeting to discuss search results and ask for suggestions from the crew.

"If the black box went down with the plane, it stands to reason that plane wreckage should be somewhere nearby, even if deep ocean currents could have shifted parts of the downed plane as it fell to the bottom," Sean said.

"Well, we have been live-streaming all our data to search headquarters for their analysis, and they should be able to tell us soon how far we need to widen this search area before we move to the location of the other ping sound," Hack interjected.

As we looked at the window a colossal squid moved across our visual field, mesmerized and confused by the lights. Unlike the giant squid, whose arms and tentacles only have suckers lined with small teeth, the colossal squid's limbs are also equipped with sharp hooks: some swiveling, others three-pointed. Its body is wider and stouter, and therefore heavier, than a giant squid's frame. Primarily inhabiting the Southern Ocean, colossal squid are believed to have longer mantles than giant squid, but shorter tentacles.

The colossal squid disappeared from view

quickly, leaving us with its powerful image burnt into our brains.

"Too bad we can't ask the squid where the wreckage is," Angela said. "Squids possess big brains and complicated nervous systems and their eyes can be as large as a foot in diameter."

"Yeah, I bet a lot of these creatures down here have swam by the wreckage and wondered what it was," I affirmed. We all took a dinner break in rotation and retired to our rooms for a few hours' sleep, before resuming our duties early the next morning.

Hatch and I continued the search in the command center, hoping for some break in the case as the rest of our crew slept. However, we saw nothing unusual until four a.m., when Hack and Sean took over watch duties and we tumbled into bed for some well-deserved rest.

It was beginning to sink in more and more that there was no plane wreckage near the first black box. We needed to move our search to the location of the other ping, where the second black box should be found. Moving quickly to the second ping site ten miles away, Eye 1 set up operations to find the second black box.

Within two hours of commencing the second black box search, Hack reported that we had found the box, lying 17,400 feet deep near a thermal vent spewing out mineral-filled steam clouds. Carefully maneuvering Eye 1 to a safe distance of 400 yards from the vent, Hatch instructed Hack to deploy Hack's Grabber to pick up the box.

Moving closely to the box from the side away from the thermal vent, Hack deployed the arm, carefully inching the business end of the arm toward the box, covered with mineralization from the vent. Easily grabbing the black box, Hack retracted the arm into the ROV and directed the unit back inside Eye 1 via the special hydraulic deployment bay.

As with the first black box, we surfaced to transfer the box to the Ocean Shield for airlift back to Washington, DC before diving again to look for wreckage. One hour later all we saw was a rock-strewn area devoid of any man-made objects. Did the bottom of the ocean swallow up the plane in some sort of earthquake scenario where the plane disappeared under slide debris?

Where was MH370? How could we find both black boxes with no wreckage nearby? When this fact got out, alien abduction of the plane would move back near the top of the list of possible disappearance scenarios, right up there with insurance fraud and a CIA cover-up.

We took a breather while awaiting news from the Federal Aviation Administration in Washington regarding flight information contained in the two black boxes. Later that afternoon, I convened a crew brainstorming session where we threw all ideas on the table to try and determine the actual location of the plane wreckage.

"I've been studying all the theories and virtually every one of them could be possible, although some theories are more likely than others," Angela said. "Specifically, I'm big on the terrorist hijacking theory, as this has been a fairly common event over the years. The question is, if MH370 was hijacked where did they land the plane? There would be some evidence or indication of a landing, no matter where they tried to land via radar, satellites, people on the ground, or dogs barking."

"I think pilot hijacking is a definite possibility," Sean chimed in. "Sure, the pilot and copilot have been checked out and they are supposedly squeaky clean, but people in the news regularly go from saints to sinners in less than one twenty-four hour news cycle. Most journalists are lazy and go for the low-hanging fruit, rather than rolling up their sleeves and digging deep into a story to get the real facts. Sure, members of the press are under severe time pressures, but in many cases they gloss over a story in a superficial way."

"Maybe the plane was accidentally shot down by United States and Thai fighter planes in a training drill that was taking place concurrently with the

MH370 disappearance and was covered up by the United States and Thailand," Hack said. "It doesn't take much to knock a commercial passenger airplane out of the sky."

"One of the most widely held theories is that a fire inside the plane killed all onboard but burned out before damaging the exterior of the plane, enabling the plane, on autopilot, to fly such a long distance before crashing into the Southern Ocean," I said.

Hatch joined the debate with, "I think Angela was trying to hitch a ride on MH370 and when her skirt came up, the pilot's hormones went into overdrive causing them to crash the plane. Fess up, Angela."

"No, you streaked in front of the cockpit windows and the horror of it put them in an uncorrectable dive," Angela retorted. "Just the tattoos on certain semi-functional parts of your anatomy are enough to invite disaster on land, sea, and air."

On the surface now in calm seas, I made a call to the FAA to see if they had any results yet on their examination of the two black boxes. I was told that the head of the FAA, Richard Byrd, would be calling us in a few minutes regarding results of their tests.

I grabbed a quick cup of coffee and waited for the call. A few moments later, Mr. Byrd's secretary was on the line transferring the call to her boss.

"Hey Plug, I have some important news for you," Mr. Byrd said. "The two black boxes you found were the same make and model as the boxes on MH370 but the serial numbers didn't match the boxes on the plane."

"You're kidding, how is this possible?" I responded.

"There was no flight data in the boxes and we guess they were activated after being dropped into the ocean by a plane or ship planting them as decoys to mislead the search for MH370," Byrd continued.

"What?" I cried out in exasperation. "We have been on a wild goose chase all this time. We are back to square one."

"Yes, it appears so," Byrd said. "We don't know what to suggest to you. Something like this has never happened before in aviation history."

Stunned, the Eye 1 crew took a collective deep breath, before this news began to sink in.

"Where do we go from here?" Hatch said, after he began to calm down.

CHAPTER TWENTY-TWO
STUMPED

I quickly made a call to Koala Dundee, who had also received the information from the FAA regarding the black boxes.

"I don't know what to think now," Dundee said. "Everyone here is blown away by this news. We all thought we were getting very close to finding MH370."

"We need to re-evaluate all search data and do some major brainstorming in order to come up with the next steps in this search," Dundee concluded.

I convened an Eye 1 crew meeting to see if there was any way we could continue to help with the MH370 search.

The consensus of the crew was that if we could no longer contribute to the MH370 search with Eye 1's unique capabilities, we should return to our Florida base to deal with the current hurricane season which was heating up quickly. A huge storm in the southern Atlantic Ocean was rapidly building up strength, promising to deliver a major punch to the Caribbean islands and possibly ravage parts of the United States mainland.

Hack said he was completing work on a new piece of software that would analyze all MH370 search data and theories in different ways that hadn't been tried to date.

"I've come up with some new search algorithms and want to try them out before we fly Eye 1 back to Florida," Hack said. "I'm calling this new software 'Detective Columbo,' to honor Peter Falk's role in the popular 1970s *Columbo* television series. And, just one more thing, if Detective Columbo finds the MH370 wreckage, all crewmembers will have to watch a *Columbo* TV marathon with me."

In preparation for our possible return to Florida to deal with the hurricane season, Angela started monitoring the tropical depression building in the Atlantic Ocean off the coast of Africa. These waters were warmer than usual, enabling the depression to gather strength earlier in its cycle.

I contacted the United States Air Force to request another ride for Eye 1 on the USAF C-5M Super Galaxy transport plane that brought us to Perth. Given their massive cargo-hauling capabilities, the C-5M Super Galaxys were very busy aircraft, primarily hauling loads of military equipment to the Afghan and Iraq theaters of war.

Everyone on the crew was shifting their focus to Eye 1's primary mission of getting in the middle of hurricanes to find out what makes them tick. We were definitely ready for our first test by fire.

The Eye 1 reality show crew was excited about the film they had in the can from our dives to find the black boxes. "We have about five episodes of material ready for editing by R.E. at his home office in Hollywood," said Jeff Huston, our onboard reality show producer. In fact, R.E. wants you to call him as soon as you can."

I phoned R.E. in Hollywood and he immediately picked up the line. "Plug, you are doing an amazing job down there," R.E. said. "I'm really surprised the black boxes turned out to be bogus decoys. This missing plane is becoming a mystery for the ages."

"Well, we haven't given up yet," I responded. "If Hack could unravel the Obamacare rollout process, I think he has a good shot at finding MH370. But we are pressed for time here as a big depression is forming off the coast of Africa headed for the Caribbean."

"As you know, we are currently editing the film of your voyage so far and will be ready to air the first shows in a couple of weeks," R.E. continued. "I think the romance between Hatch and Angela will be a big audience draw for the show along with the techno hijinks and adventure. And, if you find MH370 this will blow our ratings wide open."

"We are giving it our best shot," I said. "Don't count us out yet."

While we prepared for our return to Florida, Hatch undertook a variety of maneuvers with Eye 1 to complete our roster of tests cut short by the MH370 disaster. Our first test was a high-speed dive to see how fast the boat could move downward without causing damage to the hull and superstructure. As we shot downward at 80 mph, it felt like being at the apogee of a roller coaster ride, fear mounting to a crescendo as you almost came to a stop at the summit, before dropping like a rock down the other side, the out-of-control beast ready to leap off the track at any second.

My first and last roller coaster ride was when I was twelve years old. Shaken to the core after the big drop, my Dad, thirty-six years older than me, was totally unperturbed by the whole experience. Dad crossed the Atlantic in a troop ship in the Second World War, feeling fine as most of his shipmates were hanging over the rail or rolling around in their bunks, wishing they could die to end the pain.

The sick sensation I felt was almost the same as forty-five years before on the roller coaster, but this time I blacked out on the ride down. I don't remember any of it, but as Doc Ozz told me later, my limbs started jerking in spasms before he restrained me and I slowly regained consciousness, my breathing normalizing when we leveled off and slowed down at the bottom.

"What you experienced, Plug, was a psychogenic blackout, resulting from the stress and anxiety of the situation, not an epileptic fit," Ozz said. "Next time we dive this fast, we will have to take special measures to prevent you from having a blackout, including putting you to sleep before we dive. You will have to trust Hatch's skills controlling Eye 1 while you are asleep."

"Yeah, Plug, I wouldn't have made it through Seal training if I had a problem with something like this," Hatch said. "You can't fight when you are out."

After the dive, we performed a few more tests to ensure Eye 1 was up to the mark in her performance characteristics. We had only tested our exoskeletons briefly in a pool, and wanted to try out this new technology in the ocean environment. Our volunteers for the test were Hatch and Doc Ozz, the two best swimmers on the crew. Biologically inspired, our dolphin-based exoskeletons had the advantages of using the wearer's most powerful leg muscle groups to swim with, leaving user's hands free for other tasks. With a man or woman inside controlling the machine, the exterior of the device looked like a real dolphin, enabling it to blend in with the natural flora and fauna of the ocean.

As we cruised back toward Perth at 70 mph, we came to a stop at 500 feet depth and Hatch and Ozz exited Eye 1 in their special exoskeleton suits. Initially clumsy in the advanced apparatus, Hatch and Ozz quickly adapted their motions to optimize performance in the suits. Fish didn't pay any attention to the man-operated dolphins until Hatch and Ozz upped their speed to 25 mph. Moments later, a twenty-seven foot Great White Shark that had been lurking below them, closed in for the kill at 35 mph, the top burst speed of a Great White.

In the command center, we held our breaths, expecting our crewmates to be gobbled up any second by the ocean's apex predator. Just as the shark opened its cavernous jaws to grab Hatch, he tore away from the monster, the killer dropping behind him dramatically not being able to sustain the high speed. On land cheetahs can reach their top speed of 70 mph in three seconds, faster than most supercars, and maintain this speed for about sixty seconds, bringing down slower prey with ease.

Over the command center speakers, we could hear Hatch express a deep sigh of relief, almost shitting in his rubber drawers as Jaws had closed in on him.

"Fuck that," Hatch yelled. "It almost had me. I could feel the shark's teeth clamping around me as it prepared to digest me in one bite."

143

On deck, Angela almost fainted as our cameras showed the Great White wrapping its jaws around Hatch, preparing for its afternoon snack.

"Oh my God...Hatch!" she cried, quivering from head to toe with her eyes bugged out in disbelief.

"Are you okay, Hatch?" I called out.

"I will be okay after Angela wraps herself around me, making me forget the giant mouth that almost swallowed me whole," Hatch said.

Back aboard ship, Hatch and Ozz described what it was like to use the dolphin suits. "It was pretty amazing," Ozz said. "I felt like I was Superman, the supercharged power of my legs gave me strength I couldn't believe."

"Without the exoskeleton I would have been a tasty morsel for that shark," Hatch said. "When the Seals get these suits, they will rock."

CHAPTER TWENTY-THREE
ON THE TRAIL AGAIN

Surfacing for a full communications check, Hack ran his Detective Columbo software analyzing the latest data on the search for MH370. Hack had been playing with the software to get the broadest variety of scenarios to locate the missing plane.

"I'm getting some weird results here," Hack said. "The software is telling me that MH370 is located near Saint Paul Island in the southern Indian Ocean, one of the most remote islands in the world."

More than 1800 miles from any continent, Saint Paul Island at coordinates 38°43'48"S- 77°31'20" E is situated between Antarctica, Africa, and Australia with an area of only seven square miles and a height of 890 feet. An inactive volcano, Saint Paul Island's unusual volcanic crater is flooded and open to the sea on the east, creating an enclosed harbor with cliffs to the west rising vertically from the water.

"I am connecting to the Inmarsat Satellite

Network to get the latest photos of Saint Paul Island to see if we can spot any plane crash debris that has floated up on the shores of the island," Hack continued.

Hack streamed the photos to our command center window screen and we studied the images carefully. The view of the flooded crater harbor was dramatic, none of us having seen a geographic feature like this before. However, we couldn't spot any plane wreckage or other sign of human activity anywhere on the island except for the crumbling remains of a small stone building.

In 1889, Charles Lightoller, who later became famous as the second officer of the RMS Titanic, was shipwrecked on Saint Paul Island for eight days when the sailing barque *Holt Hill* ran aground. Lightoller speculated that pirates may have used the caves on the island to bury their treasure.

"I've run more tests on this data and confirmed that the location of MH370 is somewhere in the immediate vicinity of Saint Paul Island, I have no doubt about it," Hack concluded.

I tapped Angela on the shoulder and asked her to give me an update on the developing storm in the Southern Atlantic.

"The depression has slowed but could be upgraded to a tropical storm in the next few days," Angela said. "We need to get back there as soon as possible in order to start onsite tracking of the developing system."

"Okay," I said to Angela. "The slowing of the storm may give us some more time to find MH370 before we head back to the Caribbean."

I checked in with Koala Dundee regarding our revised plan to find MH370 based on data deciphered by Hack with his Detective Columbo software.

"Koala, we have a fix on MH370. We think it is located close to Saint Paul Island in the Southern Indian Ocean. We can be at Saint Paul Island, 2,630 miles southwest of Perth, in twenty-one hours to take a look for MH370 there, then we will head for the United States Navy base at Diego Garcia, 2,100 miles north of Saint Paul Island, to catch a ride back to Puerto Rico on the C5A Super Galaxy.

"Please proceed, Plug, we have no other viable options here. Our efforts so far have produced nothing concrete," Koala said.

Hatch dived to 500 feet and cranked Eye 1 up to full speed at 127 mph. The ride was smooth as the gas bubble around our vessel worked perfectly to enable our rapid journey to Saint Paul Island. The off-duty members of the crew rested in their quarters while Hatch and I manned the command center with the assistance of Hack working on the supercomputers.

We changed watch once with Sean and Angela before we arrived at Saint Paul Island, putting Hatch,

147

Hack, and I back on duty as we approached the island.

Surfacing just outside the flooded volcano crater, we took a sonar sounding which indicated a high tide crater entrance depth of nineteen feet, not enough room for the twenty-two foot draft of Eye 1.

The view was spectacular as we looked out from the observation deck, feeling a warm breeze coming over the steep cliffs defining the western side of the crater-harbor. I decided to send a shore party to reconnoiter the island, to see if we could spot any signs of MH370 or other related human alterations to this remote piece of land. Also, Hatch and Ozz would don their dolphin exoskeletons, to search the floor of the 600 foot deep crater-bay. The exoskeletons were fitted with special rebreather units that compensated for depth changes, preventing the bends from occurring when divers needed to surface quickly.

The dolphin exoskeletons mimicked the diving response reflex all vertebrates have, including humans, but this reflex is most strongly developed in diving animals. Whales, sharks, sea lions, and other diving vertebrates automatically slow their heart rate to conserve oxygen and send blood flow away from the muscles to the most important organs including the brain, also maintaining high levels of hemoglobin and myoglobin, which store oxygen in their blood.

Their main defense against the bends is a lung

structure that collapses under high pressure, forcing air away from the alveoli into the upper airways where gas can't enter the bloodstream, keeping blood from absorbing too much nitrogen at depth. This process also preserves a reservoir of oxygen that becomes available again during the trip back to the surface.

Diving sea animals can occasionally get the bends. Symptoms of the bends are often found in carcasses of animals that were exposed to extremely loud noise, such as naval sonar activity, or very cold water. Sonar has been linked to marine mammal deaths for a long time, though scientists don't know yet exactly how or why sonar forces them to surface too quickly.

Angela and I disembarked from the Zodiac with difficulty, the rocky volcanic shoreline of the crater causing rough footing for both of us. The camera crew had a tougher time getting on land due to the weight and awkwardness of their camera and sound equipment. Eventually, we all scrambled onto the relatively level northerly spit defining the crater entrance, with another low piece of land located on the south side of the narrow waterway. Steep cliffs rose sharply from inland portions of the crater, making upward foot access from these points almost impossible, except for rock climbers and crazy people.

After a moderate climb to the northern ridge of

the crater, we decided to walk the perimeter of the island before venturing along the slopes of the island interior.

Gazing around at spectacular views on every side, Angela remarked, "This is absolutely beautiful, I can't believe a place like this exists. I don't see any sign of MH370."

I concurred, noting the steep cliffs down to the rocky shoreline of the island, marking a sharp contrast between land and sea.

Crossing a rise, we were immediately taken aback as a rookery of Rockhopper penguins appeared before our eyes, banding together in tight formation for protection. Their relatively calm behavior indicated they had seen humans before and were accustomed to our presence.

Completing our circuit of the island without noting anything unusual, we walked along the ridge of the crater back to our starting point. At 880 feet elevation the top of the island allowed magnificent perspectives of the crater, an observer's first thought being that a large meteorite had created the big hole rather than a collapsing volcano.

Our surface inspection of the island striking out with no evidence of MH370, we wondered if Hatch and Ozz had found out anything on their extended dive to the bottom of the crater. As our Zodiac came into view, we saw Hatch and Ozz sitting by the launch, both men intensely scrutinizing Ozz's laptop.

Hatch and Angela hugged and French kissed with Angela saying, "I missed you, Frogman, I thought sharks might get you down there. I want Froggy to play with me in my bathtub tonight."

Grinning at Angela's remarks, Hatch said, "Did you landlubbers find anything? We've got some big news for you guys."

"Nada," I said. "We found absolutely nothing to indicate a plane had crashed anywhere near here. This may turn out to be another wild goose chase."

"You are so wrong," Hatch responded. "We hit the jackpot, take a look at this."

I sat down beside Hatch and carefully cradled the laptop between my thighs, before taking a close look at the screen.

Most of the screen image was dark but in the center of the screen lit up brightly by LED camera lights was a two foot diameter metal rod connected to a huge hydraulic mechanism protruding out of the bottom of the crater at 300 feet deep.

"What is this?" I asked Hatch.

"We found one of these mechanisms at each corner of the crater bottom, comprising a four-sided rectangle measuring 1,500 feet on the longest sides and 250 feet wide," Hatch said. "Also, we noticed six-inch wide straight line gaps in the crater defining the outline of the rectangle. It appears that someone

151

has constructed a device down there of massive proportions, for what purpose I do not know. The asphalt-covered surface of the rectangle is perfectly level and looks like an airport runway.

"We took some readings with an advanced underwater version of Cavefinder, a specialized void-finding technology that can precisely detect caves and other underground cavities," Ozz said. "With Cavefinder we determined there was a 200 foot deep void directly under the rectangle."

"Who would come to a remote island like this and go to great expense and effort to build some kind of cave under a water-filled crater?" I interjected. "This doesn't make any sense. Perhaps we should take Cavefinder and see if there are any other caves on the island."

I asked Hatch and Ozz to take Cavefinder measurements around the entire island while Angela and I went back to Eye 1 to examine data Hatch and Ozz had collected so far and check with Hack for his assessment of this information. Ozz had already live-streamed the data to Hack, who was reviewing it on the Eye 1 supercomputers.

Angela and I boarded the Zodiac for our trip back to Eye 1, while the reality show camera crew stayed with Hatch and Ozz to follow their movements around the island.

Back onboard Eye 1, Angela and I immediately

met with Hack in the command center. Hack was happy that we got back safe and sound from our shore mission. "My analysis of the data confirms Hatch and Doc Ozz's description of the underwater rectangular structure appearing like a typical airport runway, except that this runway is 300 feet underwater with a deep void underneath it, housing a mammoth hydraulic apparatus that is used to raise the runway hundreds of feet to a point about fifty feet above the surface of the water," Hack said. "I calculated this Saint Paul Island runway to be only 1,500 feet long, at best a landing strip for small STOL-Short Takeoff and Landing planes."

STOL aircraft are equipped with landing gear and brakes optimized for unprepared airstrips. These features usually include strong A-frame construction and powerful shock absorbers in the landing gear to adjust for the rapid landing descent. Further, the aerodynamic design specifications of STOL aircraft and advanced onboard avionics enable crews to optimize the flight profile in approach and takeoff. In contrast, typical large passenger jets require a minimum of 6,000 feet to land safely.

"Somebody has gone to great expense and effort to install this unique landing strip," I said. "What could its purpose be and where are the people that operate this runway?"

Hatch and Ozz tramped into the command

153

center after completing their circuit of Saint Paul Island with the Cavefinder device. Both men were tired after their long dive and Cavefinder survey.

"Let's get a couple of cups of coffee and something to eat, before we brief you on what we found," Hatch said. "I'm as hungry as a bear."

Thirty minutes later, Hatch and Ozz reappeared in the command center looking refreshed and ready to explain their findings.

"Okay guys," Hatch said. "At first we didn't believe it but after taking multiple measurements at different locations, we determined there is a large man-made structure under the center of the island with a symmetrical design containing a number of floors going well below sea level."

"We found no signs of any access or egress points to this underground structure, but there must be a way in," Hatch continued. "I want to go in there to see what is going on."

"How are we going to get in there if you couldn't find any access points?" I asked.

"I think we are going to have to dive under the island where the runway is and see what we can find," Hatch said. "We didn't have enough time on our first dive down there to take a close look at everything."

"I'm up for it," said Ozz, groaning and stretching after the day's heavy workout with Hatch. "But not right now. I need a good hot bath and rest tonight and will be ready for the dive tomorrow morning."

CHAPTER TWENTY-FOUR
IN DEEP

We conferred about the risks involved in Hatch and Ozz diving to the bottom of the crater-lake again. After all, no one onboard knew who was behind this massive construction work on such a remote island, or what their motives were for undertaking this unusual project. I said we should immediately contact the US Navy on Diego Garcia, to make them aware of what has happened on Saint Paul Island, and alert our other United States defense department contacts about this situation.

"We have to take serious safety precautions here," I told the crew. "Our mission searching for MH370 is peaceful but it is possible a belligerent party could be behind this extensive underground construction activity. We can't take any chances."

Crewmembers affirmed this strategy with nods and yeas. No one wanted to risk lives in these unpredictable circumstances. Military backup may be needed.

Captain Nimitz, commander of United States naval forces on Diego Garcia, took my call and I informed him of what we had learned so far on Saint Paul Island.

"You can't be serious about this, Plug, we do regular overflights of Saint Paul Island and have never noticed anything like this going on there," Nimitz said. "I suggest that Eye 1 back away a safe distance from the island, while we move some intelligence assets over there to see what is going on. We have a nuclear submarine in the neighborhood and will send some reconnaissance planes over there to take a look. Saint Paul Island is a French protectorate, so I will call our French allies to advise them of the situation and get their approval and cooperation for whatever actions we may need to take. The French will probably deploy some of their assets once they know what is happening on Saint Paul Island."

As Eye 1 backed away from Saint Paul Island, we dropped toward the bottom at 3,000 feet to take some scans and sensor readings of the underbelly of the island, hoping to gather more information about the puzzling underground structure located there.

At 500 feet depth we stopped momentarily to allow Hack to get the best readings possible. Hack had a serious look on his face as he reviewed his findings.

"I have detected a large circular hole dug into the center of the island at 350 feet under water," Hack said. "To make this hole they must have used a large specialized tunneling machine similar to the digger that built the Chunnel under the English Channel a few years ago. I can only guess at what the purpose of this underwater channel is, one possibility is that submarines could enter a dock under the island without being detected on the surface."

"I will immediately relay this information to Captain Nimitz," I said. "Nimitz said he would directly inform us of the results of the Navy reconnaissance missions."

At ten miles from Saint Paul Island, we rose to a depth of fifty feet below the surface, so we would remain undetected by any observation post on the island, and could deploy our communications aerials above the surface.

I checked with Angela regarding the current status of the large tropical storm heading toward the Caribbean from the Cape Verde Islands off the west coast of Africa.

"This storm, now called Hurricane Rage, has sustained wind speeds of 78 mph, making it a Category 1 hurricane," Angela said. "It is now 1,700 miles east of the Caribbean Sea travelling at a speed of about 12 mph across the Southern Atlantic Ocean. Projected landfall is six to seven days from now at

Puerto Rico. If Hurricane Rage keeps on this course, it will hit the Florida Keys in nine days. We need to make haste to Diego Garcia so we can catch our flight to Puerto Rico and get into this hurricane."

After a quick lunch I went back to the command center where Captain Nimitz was waiting on the line for me. "Plug, I have some interesting news for you. We have confirmed your information about the large structure underneath Saint Paul Island and the access hole to this structure 350 feet below the surface of the ocean. I have communicated this information to our French allies and we have agreed to jointly conduct a detailed onsite inspection of the island early tomorrow morning."

"Okay Captain," I said. "Do you want any of Eye 1's crew to assist you and the French with your inspection tomorrow?"

"No, we are concerned about the security risk for you civilians," Nimitz continued. "Although I understand you have an ex-Navy Seal on your crew, he is welcome to join us in the morning."

Hatch immediately agreed to assist in the inspection and asked Nimitz where he should meet them on the island.

"Meet us at the entrance of the crater bay at 0700," Nimitz responded.

Early the next morning Hatch shut down the Zodiac motor and beached the vessel at the same spot as the day before. A large contingent of United States and French naval personnel greeted Hatch with French Navy Commander Henri Napoleon in command of the inspection party.

"Hatch, can you give the group a briefing on what Eye 1 has found out about this island so far?" Napoleon said.

Hatch reviewed the information Eye 1 had gathered about the island, and concluded, "We have found no indication whatsoever of MH370 on Saint Paul Island, which our Detective Columbo software indicated was the location of the MH370 wreckage."

A French naval commando, the French equivalent of a US Navy Seal, quickly stepped forward and said, "We have a mini-sub available for close inspection of the crater bay and the outer perimeter of the island. Would you like to come with us on this mission?"

Hatch quickly agreed to the offer and Commander Napoleon divided the group for various missions around the island.

The mini-sub dropped to the bottom of the crater bay and soon discovered the huge structure Hatch had referred to that had been built into the bottom of the bay. The French naval commandos onboard the mini-sub were incredulous upon viewing the giant hydraulic-powered landing strip hidden at the bottom of the crater.

"Mon Dieu!" French Naval Commando George

Picard exclaimed. "I can't believe this."

Cameras and sensors aboard the mini-sub took detailed readings and photographs of the underwater device, the LED lights of the sub brightly illuminating every detail of the unusual machine. No movement or other activity by any part of the underwater airstrip belied its usage and capabilities.

After the mini-sub's inspection of the crater bay, it moved out through the narrow bay entrance and began examining the outside of Saint Paul Island. Nothing appeared out of the ordinary, so the French commander of the mini-sub, Lieutenant De Gaulle, decided to enter the round access tunnel 350 feet below the surface of the ocean.

Conferring with Hatch, the only civilian on the mini-sub, Hatch readily assented to Lieutenant De Gaulle's plan of entering the tunnel.

Before venturing into the tunnel, Lieutenant De Gaulle also conferred with Captain Napoleon, who was completing his inspection on the surface of Saint Paul Island.

"Lieutenant, I want you to enter the tunnel after our surface inspection party returns to our ships," Captain Napoleon said, referring to the French destroyer and US Navy nuclear sub patrolling Indian Ocean waters around the small island.

161

CHAPTER TWENTY-FIVE
TUNNEL OF LOVE

The go-ahead finally given to the mini-sub by Captain Napoleon, Lieutenant De Gaulle eased the mini-sub into the tunnel entrance, the walls of the perfectly round tunnel reflecting the exterior hull lights of the little sub, with plenty of room to spare for the small vessel.

Onboard the mini-sub, Hatch and the five French commandos nervously watched and waited as they proceeded deeper into the tunnel, not knowing what would happen next.

Nearing the center of Saint Paul Island, lights coming from somewhere further along the tunnel, created a bright scene in front of the sub, the outline of the tunnel giving way to a large cavern-like opening that rose several hundred feet in front of them above the water. Moments later the mini-sub bobbed to the surface, revealing a huge underground dock facility that appeared to be designed to handle large submarines.

Hatch and the French commandos clambered out of the sub onto the large concrete floor area surrounding the water-filled dock enclosure.

Immediately, a large number of machine gun equipped soldiers in black uniforms sprang from every side, quickly encircling the mini-sub crew who stood gaping in surprise at the scene unfolding around them. Next, as Hatch and the commandos looked back toward the tunnel they had just come out of, a giant gate clanged shut completely blocking the tunnel. The mini-sub had no way out now, her crew a captive pawn of these strange occupants of the underground island chamber.

"Put your hands up and lay down on the floor with your legs and arms spread apart. Don't try anything or we will kill you right now," said a tall Korean soldier in command of the armed detail. "Who are you and what are you doing here?" the Korean continued.

Lieutenant De Gaulle responded quickly, saying, "We are French sailors inspecting a French protectorate. What are you doing here on French soil? You have no permission to be here."

The black-clad soldiers menacingly pointed their guns at Hatch and company while their leader exhorted, "You are now our prisoners and keep your mouths shut until you are told otherwise."

Hatch and the French Navy men were escorted to a barred cell via a corridor leading off from the dock chamber.

Onboard the *Lafayette*, Captain Napoleon was told that communications with the mini-sub had been cut off, and nothing was known of the current disposition of the sub or its crew.

Raising the alarm, Captain Napoleon immediately contacted Captain Billings, the commander of United States Nuclear Submarine Shark, and Plug on Eye 1.

"We have a situation here, gentlemen, and we have to proceed carefully or the mini-sub crew will be lost," Napoleon said.

Both Captain Billings and Plug agreed with Captain Napoleon's assessment, Plug saying, "Yes, we will have to tread carefully here until we know what is going on."

Under the island in their cell, Hatch and the French commandos finally received food and drink from their Korean guards and tried to converse with them to find out when they would be released. The Koreans said they could not talk with the prisoners and quickly left.

Hatch had noticed on the way to their cell that the lighting in the halls was fairly primitive, the Koreans using old-fashioned incandescent light bulbs to light their way. Also, he observed that the Kalashnikov machine guns the Koreans were carrying were old

Soviet issue AK-47s the Viet Cong had used in the Vietnam War. The South Korean military used US manufactured weapons, suggesting their captors were members of the North Korean armed forces.

Hatch and the French commandos speculated about the purpose of North Korea building an elaborate hidden facility on a remote uninhabited island but couldn't come up with any reasonable explanation, except that it could be a launch site for North Korean nuclear missiles.

Back on Eye 1, Hack continued examining all data and readings from Saint Paul Island and discovered an Internet hot spot on the island. Checking his instrumentation and software, Hack determined the hot spot was transmitting and receiving information via a North Korean communications satellite parked in a geosynchronous orbit over Saint Paul Island.

"I have been able to unlock and access the hot spot signal," Hack said, "but I can't yet figure out what information the North Koreans on the island are sending and receiving via the hot spot satellite connection. They embed their coded signals in Facebook and Twitter messages so that these communications cannot be intercepted. I will have to write some more code for the Detective Columbo software so it can unravel these messages."

"Please keep at it, Hack," I said. "I want you to patch this information directly over to the *Lafayette* and Shark as they may be of help in deciphering these messages."

"I doubt it, but I will send them the information as I get it," Hack continued. "Eye 1 communications technology is light-years ahead of current US and French military communications systems. We make state of the art look like old school."

After consulting with his superiors in France and Captain Billings brass at the Pentagon, Captain Napoleon was ordered to direct a shore party of French and US Special Forces teams to land on Saint Paul Island and find a way into the underground fortress. Hack called Captain Napoleon to tell him that the best place to initially look for access to the belowground chamber was at the Wi-Fi hot spot Hack had identified.

Also, the Pentagon ordered aircraft carrier *USS George H.W. Bush* to travel to Saint Paul Island to provide support for any military operations needed to help secure the island back to French control.

The French Foreign Ministry contacted North Korea regarding their illegal presence on Saint Paul Island, receiving no response from the world's most bizarre and unpredictable totalitarian regime. Experts differed on whether North Korea had the capability to launch intercontinental ballistic missiles that could reach the United States mainland.

On Saint Paul Island, French and US shore parties

quickly found the Wi-Fi hot spot on the highest ridge of the island overlooking the crater bay as per GPS coordinates supplied by Hack. The Wi-Fi hot spot satellite communications apparatus was built into the lava so it couldn't be spotted from the air. Closer examination of the equipment and immediate vicinity, revealed a round hatch cover. The Special Forces team attempted to open the hatch with some small pry tools they had with them, but the hatch didn't budge.

Lieutenant De Gaulle ordered the operators to blow the hatch open using C4 plastic explosives which all elite Special Forces troops were trained in using. After the charge was inserted around the hatch, De Gaulle ordered everyone to move back a safe distance so the radio detonated explosive could do its work without hurting anyone.

"Fire in the hole!" De Gaulle exclaimed just prior to the explosion which blew off the hatch, revealing a ladder-equipped tunnel heading straight down into the bowels of the island, with occasional incandescent lamps lighting the way downward.

De Gaulle ordered four Special Forces operators, two French and two Americans, to climb down the ladder and find out what was at the bottom of the tunnel. The operators were told to return fire only if engaged, minimizing the possibility of potential harm to the captives below by the North Koreans.

CHAPTER TWENTY-SIX
CODE BROKEN

Meanwhile, back on Eye 1, Hack was making progress decoding the North Korean Facebook and Twitter messages with the newly updated Detective Columbo software.

"I have broken their code and can intercept messages they are sending back to North Korea in real time," Hack shouted. "I will project these messages on the big screen for everyone to see."

Immediately appearing on our front window-viewing screen were North Korean words with their English translations appearing below courtesy of Google translate.

"Level 4 alert, our facility has been breached by French and American forces. They are climbing down the tunnel from the Wi-Fi hot spot. What are your orders?"

"Lock the door at the bottom of the tunnel and station soldiers there in case the French and

Americans blow it open," the North Korean message continued. "Await further instructions."

"I have now decoded all North Korean messages for the past year," Hack said. "There is some very interesting stuff here. I think we should call Captain Napoleon and have him put a hold on military operations on the island until we know what the North Koreans are up to."

I immediately picked up the phone and told Captain Napoleon about the decoded messages we had uncovered, and he agreed to order Special Forces out of the tunnel and maintain their position on the ridge. I also informed Captain John Paul Jones on the aircraft carrier USS George H.W. Bush and Captain Billings on the submarine USS Shark, of this turn of events and they said they would relay the information to the Pentagon.

Everyone in the command center gazed up at the screen and saw hundreds of messages that had passed between Pyongyang, the North Korean capital, and the North Korean bunker facility on Saint Paul Island.

Hack was quickly reading the messages and highlighted those of great significance in larger type. The first highlighted message stated: "We want no indications on the surface of Saint Paul Island that there is work going on underneath the island and the crater bay. Be very careful in this regard. Anything we do aboveground could be picked up by satellites."

The next message read: "We need the project to be completed on schedule by November 30 so that the rest of our plan can be put in place. Our Dear Leader will then visit the island via submarine to make sure everything is ready. It better be finished or heads will roll."

The crew digested these messages, before reading further.

"We have received confirmation of the identity of our package and the flight he will be on. Plans are now being made to hijack the plane and divert it to Saint Paul Island. A communications blackout is now in effect and the Wi-Fi hotspot will only be turned on briefly at random times every few days to communicate important messages."

Everyone in the command center looked at each other and I exclaimed, "They are referring to Flight MH370. We need to know the identity of the package."

All messages had been relayed to Captain Jones on the USS George H.W. Bush, Lafayette Captain Napoleon, and USS Shark Captain Billings. Also, the information was sent immediately to the Pentagon and the CIA and French Intelligence.

The crew was abuzz with conversation and I took a call from Chairman of the Joint Chiefs of Staff, Admiral Peter "Popeye" Williams. "Plug, we need to find out ASAP the identity of the package. To that end, we request that Hack tie his investigation directly in with intelligence analysts at the Pentagon, CIA, and French Intelligence. Not a moment can be wasted; our national security is at stake here."

I affirmed to Admiral Williams that Eye 1 would proceed promptly to act upon his request, and I told him that all care and restraint would be taken on Saint Paul Island to prevent the situation from blowing up in our face.

In their cell on the island, Hack and French Special Forces team members were growing more anxious by the minute about possible events taking place outside their cell. Fed regularly by their North Korean captors and allowed to wash and shave, Hack and company still could not communicate with their North Korean guards, some who spoke English as per the mini-sub crew's initial contact with the North Koreans.

Worried sick about Hatch, Angela was tied up in knots. "Those North Koreans better not hurt him or I will personally go after the Dear Leader," Angela said. "We have checked the MH370 passenger manifest and found a man that could be the package," Hack said. "It is quantum computing expert Mr. X, a CIA operative who is known only to brass in the Pentagon and CIA personnel with top security clearance. Mr. X was likely on a secret mission to China to gain information about China's quantum computing research program, which, if successful, would enable China to dominate the world's cyberspace with drastic implications for national security, business, and a host of other critical fields."

"In its infancy, quantum computing is the next big thing in computer technology, exponentially faster than current supercomputers with the ability to break all cryptographic codes and control cyberspace," Hack continued. "Quantum computers are different from existing digital computers based on transistors; whereas digital computers require data to be encoded into binary digits-*bits*-each of which is always in one of two definite states 0 or 1, quantum computing uses subatomic quantum bits, which can be in an infinite variety of states at the same time. This variety of states characteristic of quantum computing, known as superposition, enables all calculations, however complex, to be solved virtually instantly."

President Tripp called French President Eiffel to discuss this urgent crisis. "We must act quickly or it will be a calamity if North Korea acquires quantum computing technology," President Tripp said. President Eiffel agreed with his American counterpart, stating, "We need to get Mr. X back, to prevent the North Koreans from breaking Mr. X, causing him to reveal his extensive quantum computing knowledge. That would be disastrous for the entire world community."

In their prison cell, Hatch and the French Special Forces operators were frantically trying to escape their confinement. Hatch and his fellow captors had been chipping away at the bottom of one wall with a spoon that was in a meal tray, the missing spoon not being detected by the guards. The men were very careful when they worked on the hole, only digging when the guards were elsewhere on their rounds.

Hatch was taking his turn working on the hole, when the spoon finally broke through the wall, exposing a narrow passageway on the outside of their cell, barely wide enough for a person to crawl through.

Expanding the hole in the next several days, the men hid the hole from the guards by working under one of the crude beds captives slept on. While expanding the hole to a size that men could crawl through, Hatch and company discussed what they would do when they got out of their cell into the passageway.

"I think that only one of us should initially escape down the passageway, so that the others can keep up the facade that everyone is still in the cell," Hatch said. "And given that I am the only person here that has reconnoitered the surface of the island and the crater bay, I think I should be the one to attempt an escape out the hole."

The suggestion was well received by the other men except for Lieutenant De Gaulle, who responded, "The problem, Hatch, is that you are a civilian and shouldn't be risking your neck; putting ourselves in harm's way is our job as special operators."

"I'm not worried about that," Hatch replied. "There is too much at stake here for someone who doesn't know the lay of the land to attempt the mission."

Lieutenant De Gaulle reluctantly agreed, enabling Hatch to make preparations for his escape. One hour later Hatch slithered through the hole into the passageway, scraping his back as he squeezed through the jagged-edged cavity. Once into the tight corridor, Hatch could feel a slight breeze coming up the passage from the left, his nostrils picking up the smell of salty sea air.

Hatch wriggled along for several hundred feet before he came to the end of the passageway, capped off by a camouflaged cover, enabling air to come in the venting corridor but making the hole invisible to people viewing the vent on the outside.

Pushing the bottom of the vent cover out about two feet, Hatch gaped at the two hundred foot drop to the crater-bay below. Quickly realizing his only way to escape was to dive into the bay, Hatch prepared himself for the big drop. Launching himself into the air, Hatch rolled into the classic swan dive used by famous Acapulco cliff divers for decades. Jumping was too risky, as feet first impact can be lethal due to explosive rupture of the large colon. But a dive from several hundred feet high is at the outer limits of the capabilities of any humans, including professional high divers.

Hatch carefully arced his dive, his outpointed hands slicing through the water allowing his perfectly vertical body to make the smallest water disturbance as he plunged into the crater-bay. Hatch lucked out as he entered the water, catching the top of a wave thereby minimizing the impact.

Hatch went down deep before rising to the surface and gasping for air as he looked around the crater-bay. He saw nothing while swimming toward the ocean entrance to the bay with long rhythmic strokes, climbing onto the northern spit of land where they had beached the zodiac a few days previously.

Chilled by the swim, Hatch shivered for a few minutes before warming up slowly in the bright sunshine. How was he going to contact Eye 1, Hatch thought, as he deliberated his next course of action.

Circling overhead, a US Navy unmanned drone remotely controlled by sailors on the USS George H.W. Bush Aircraft Carrier, spotted Hatch and live-streamed the video back to the carrier. Quickly alerted about the revealing footage, Carrier Commander Captain Jones quickly called Plug on Eye 1 to alert him that Hatch was okay.

"That is great news, Captain," Plug said to Captain Jones. "How are we going to get Hatch out of there?"

"I will contact Captain Billings on the USS Shark nuclear sub to send in a Seal underwater insertion team to pick up Hatch," Captain Billings replied.

CHAPTER TWENTY-SEVEN
INTERNATIONAL INCIDENT

Back in Washington, Joint Chiefs Chairman Popeye Williams conferred with his French counterpart, Defense Minister OnGarde about resolving the situation before all hell broke loose on the island. Chairman Williams said they could insert sleeping gas into the underground chamber to put the North Koreans to sleep, prior to storming the underground facility. The special sleeping gas, also known as "knockout gas," would not hurt anyone, putting them to sleep for about twelve hours. Recently developed for the US military, this new sleeping gas was absorbed through the skin, rendering gas masks totally ineffective.

President Tripp and French President Eiffel quickly agreed to use the sleeping gas and directed military forces to deploy the gas as soon as possible in the underground cavern on Saint Paul Island.

The sleeping gas, known as "nighty-night," was

loaded at MacDill Air Force Base in Florida on a new GPS-guided rocket called *Wile E. Coyote,* capable of speeds in excess of 10,000 miles per hour. One hour later, the *Wile E. Coyote* craft automatically turned off its engines over the Indian Ocean and deployed a special GPS-equipped, thruster-guided parachute, landing minutes later in the ocean several miles from the USS George Bush.

The high-speed stealth helicopter used in the successful Osama Bin Laden raid in Pakistan, the MH-X Stealth Black Hawk, quickly picked up the nighty-night sleeping gas container and brought it back to the carrier.

Back on Eye 1 after Navy Seals picked him up from Saint Paul Island, Hatch and Angela had a rambunctious reunion in Hatch's cabin. Surfacing in the command center one hour later, Hatch glowed after the delicious lovemaking performed contrary to orders, but quickly got down to business updating me regarding the situation on the island.

"I want to get my buddies off the island as soon as possible," Hatch told me. "They are in grave peril."

I filled Hatch in on plans to gas the island chamber in order to rescue the captive special operators and find out what was happening on the island.

On Saint Paul Island the joint team of US and French Special Forces were roping down the sides of the summit inserting nighty-night gas canisters into vent pipes and sealing vents with duct-taped camo plastic sheeting.

After inserting nighty-night gas canisters into vents and sealing vent entrances, the special operators roped back up to the summit to await further orders.

Sensors had been placed around the island to detect human movement in the underground bunker. Prior to insertion of the nighty-night canisters, considerable human activity had been recorded around the clock in the man-made cavern. As the nighty-night gas worked its way around the illicit structure, seamen on the USS George Bush monitoring the sensors observed a steady decline in human movement on their large flat-screen computer monitors.

Two hours later, sensor monitors reported no movement in the bunker. Military brass on ships and submarines near Saint Paul Island alerted me to the situation and conferred with the Pentagon and French Defense Ministry about the next course of action.

It was determined that special operators on the summit of Saint Paul Island would climb down the ladder into the facility to determine effects of the nighty-night gas on North Korean personnel in the bunker. Entering the underground chamber from the bottom of the surface access tunnel, United States and French Special Forces members were stunned

179

by what they saw. North Korean troops were laying everywhere in a variety of body positions, still breathing, but totally immobilized in every other respect.

Moving through the facility, operators observed the same situation everywhere, hundreds of people temporarily out for the count. Their first priority was to find Special Forces personnel who were held captive along with Hatch, before he escaped with his death-defying dive into the crater-bay.

On one of the floors near the top of the underground structure, operators found several barred rooms resembling jail cells. Looking into the cells via barred windows in the doors, the men quickly identified the cell containing the captured Special Forces soldiers. Using a small C4 charge taped to the jail cell door lock, access was quickly gained to the detention chamber.

The five captives were splayed out in various positions in the beds and on the floor, as if they had been flash-frozen in place by the quick-acting nighty-night gas. The question was how to get the sleeping prisoners out of the bunker as fast as possible before the North Koreans woke up.

Captain Napoleon on the French Destroyer Lafayette, quickly radioed his superiors requesting more troops to secure the facility before the North Koreans awakened, and to get the captives back on nearby Naval ships for medical treatment and debriefing. French and American commanders decided that eight platoons of Special Forces operators, two French platoons and two American platoons totaling 184 men and 16 women, would take control of the North Korean facility. Women were increasingly active in elite military combat forces around the world, demonstrating that females could kick serious ass along with men.

One squad of operators was tasked with opening the underwater access door in the below sea level docking facility where the French mini-sub was imprisoned since Hatch and company were captured. Once this door was open, the mini-sub could exit the chamber into the Indian Ocean and other friendly mini-subs could enter the docking facility as needed.

Another squad of Special Forces operators was charged with searching the deepest recesses of the gigantic underground bunker. This detachment, led by French Lieutenant Clouseau, exited the elevator at the lowest level, a large open room with a high ceiling. Stepping out of the elevator, Lieutenant Clouseau observed a few gassed North Koreans lying in different locations around the room and exclaimed, "What is that plane doing here? I can't believe it!"

CHAPTER TWENTY-EIGHT
PAYDIRT

Standing tall in the center of the room, a huge airliner commanded the space, dominating the scene and totally surprising the French soldiers. Walking around the plane and carefully examining the aircraft's markings, Lieutenant Clouseau let out a yell: "This is Malaysian airliner MH370; we have found it!" Clouseau quickly radioed this information to his superiors, who in turn contacted the Americans and Plug on Eye 1.

Receiving the message in the command center on Eye 1, Plug was overjoyed at the news. He jumped up and down shouting, *We did it, we did it!* Other crewmembers joined in the celebration, Hatch and Angela dancing around, tightly intertwined.

Plug called Captain John Paul Jones, on the carrier USS George H.W. Bush, requesting permission to take an Eye 1 team into the North Korean facility to see MH370.

Meanwhile, back on Paul Island, French, and American special operators were positioning themselves around the underground bunker to round up North Koreans when they woke up in a couple of hours from their nighty night gas-induced slumber.

North Korean officials in Pyongyang were noticeably tight-lipped as events unfolded on Saint Paul Island, North Korea, caught with its pants down, their illegal incursion on French territory exposed. French and United States governments were keeping a tight lid on developments on Saint Paul Island, not wanting to disclose information to the press prior to resolution of the destabilizing international incident.

Entering the unusual underground plane hangar, Plug, Hatch, and Hack were part of an international delegation of government officials, military personnel, and investigators charged with the task of determining how and why Malaysian Airlines Flight MH370 ended up under Saint Paul Island.

Before the international group arrived at Saint Paul Island, forensic investigators had combed through the interior and exterior of the plane to identify fingerprints, fibers, and markings that would help explain circumstances around MH370's hijacking. In the cockpit, investigators examined instrument panels and the plane's computer system to obtain clues about how the plane was taken and diverted to Saint Paul Island.

The investigation would take several weeks but some facts related to the disappearance were already clear. The North Koreans had taken charge of MH370 and diverted it away from the intended destination of Peking. The hijacked plane landed on the ingenious runway that rose out of the Saint Paul Island crater-bay and tilted up as the plane landed, causing it to slow down quickly on the short runway surface, MH370 losing a wing flaperon in the hair-raising first-of-a-kind landing. The flaperon had not been found and must have floated back out into the Indian Ocean where currents moved it far from Saint Paul Island.

No sign was yet found of MH370's passengers who would have survived the ordeal. Did the North Koreans kill them, or were they held prisoner somewhere on the island? Also, it was possible that the North Koreans had moved MH370's occupants back to North Korea. And what about the disposition of the package, Mr. X, the American quantum computing genius whose capture was the purpose of the unusual North Korean operation? If never found, the lost plane would permanently mask the true cause of MH370's disappearance, enabling the North Koreans to use the quantum computing intelligence coup for their various nefarious activities. The world would think Mr. X went down with the plane.

Entering the Saint Paul Island underground chamber where MH370 was held, the international group marveled at how the plane could have ended up in this location, under an island in the middle of the Indian Ocean.

Hatch commented, "I don't believe this," while Hack enjoined, "The technical wizardry involved in this operation is mind-boggling."

The international investigatory group was led around the outside of the plane, before taking turns viewing the inside of MH370 from the plane entrance at the top of the stairs. It was important that nothing was disturbed inside the plane which could compromise getting accurate information in the investigation. Too many crime scenes, including the O.J. Simpson murder case, were tainted by mishandling of evidence and other mistakes by investigating police officers. In fact, some said the O.J. Simpson case taught police what not to do at a crime scene and was later used as the basis for reforms in LAPD police investigative procedures.

Completing their tour of MH370, investigators met to plan further data and evidence collection activities, before returning to their vessels anchored off Saint Paul Island.

As the North Koreans woke up, French and American special operators herded them to a large auditorium in the center of the structure, and prepared for interrogating the prisoners to determine what had been going on in the illegal installation. The prisoners were agitated and upset at being captured in their secret compound.

Hatch reunited with the French special operators who were held captive with him prior to his amazing escape dive into the Saint Paul Island crater-bay. These men were still shaking off effects of the nighty-night gas.

"Wakey, wakey, you guys," Hatch exclaimed, before shaking hands and backslapping his friends who had been captured with him by the North Koreans.

Now the crime scene was under control, attention focused on finding the passengers of MH370 including quantum computing expert Mr. X, in the event they were still held captive on Saint Paul Island.

To assist this phase of the search, the special CaveFinder machine was brought into the bunker to locate sections of the facility that had not yet been found.

North Korea was in the hot seat at the United Nations, with France protesting North Korea's illegal seizure of French territory. Other allies of France, including the United States, joined the call to place more sanctions on North Korea to further limit development of nuclear weapons by the rogue regime.

Activating CaveFinder in the lowest known level of the bunker, the machine scanned rock structures underneath the facility, probing for another man-made chamber. Nothing was found until CaveFinder looked at adjacent rock formations near the main bunker.

American technical specialist Lieutenant Black furrowed his brow while examining the Cavefinder LED monitor screen, closely studying the lines and shapes appearing before him.

"I think I have it!" Lieutenant Black exclaimed. "There is a perfectly square chamber horizontally 100 feet away from the main chamber, both underground spaces connected by a narrow passageway."

"I can see considerable human movement in the lowest chamber, indicating that several hundred people are located on the four levels of the square void," Black continued.

Lieutenant Black radioed this information to commanders of Naval vessels circling Saint Paul Island, who immediately conferred with each other and teleconferenced with top military officials in Washington and Paris.

On Eye 1 we were all excited to receive this information, hoping beyond hope that the MH370 passengers were being held in the previously undiscovered chamber.

North Korean soldiers in the newly discovered

chamber had probably been alerted by their counterparts in the main cavern prior to the nighty night gas taking full effect on them, quickly sealing off the newly identified chamber from the knockout gas. This caused French and American commanders to tread carefully in their efforts to gain access to the new chamber.

Communications were initiated between French and United States troops in the main chamber with inhabitants of the recently discovered square void, via a North Korean internal intercom system. Korean interpreters had recently been flown in by France and the United States to handle language problems between the opposing forces.

North Koreans in the square chamber were given the ultimatum of surrendering peacefully or being put to sleep by nighty night gas.

Knowing they were cornered on all sides, residents of the square chamber elected to surrender to French and United States forces.

As inhabitants streamed out of the tunnel from the square chamber to the main bunker, French, United States, and Malaysian officials were greeted by cries of exultation by prisoners who indicated they had been on Flight MH370.

"Thank you, thank you, thank you, we thought we would never get out of here!" exclaimed MH370 Captain Zaharie Ahmad Shah, leader of the

EYE OF THE HURRICANE 1

procession out of the deep prison bunker. Former MH370 passengers behind Captain Shah also joined in the chorus of relief and excitement at being freed from their weeks-long captivity. Captain Shah and most of the passengers looked to be in good health after their abduction by the North Koreans, who had taken control of MH370 before the ill-fated flight was diverted in the opposite direction to its original route from Kuala Lumpur, Malaysia, to Peking, China.

At the end of the long line of people vacating the prison bunker, a middle-aged man in ragged clothing limped into the main bunker displaying signs of extreme hunger with many cuts, lacerations, and bruises over his entire body, suggesting he had been severely tortured by his North Korean captors.

Identifying the injured man as Mr. X, the American quantum computing genius, French and United States military intelligence officers quickly led him away from the main group for special debriefing regarding his ordeal in the hands of the ruthless North Koreans. These Intel officers were desperate to know if Mr. X had been broken by the North Koreans, revealing top secret classified information about quantum technology. This would enable North Korea to take the lead in cyber-hacking, causing destabilization of the world's economy and disruption of national security across the globe.

Families of MH370 passengers, who had mostly

DEAN LANDERS

given up on ever seeing their loved ones again, were overjoyed when they received news their lost relatives had been found and were okay.

Once the press picked up the story that MH370 had been found with passengers alive, the good news flashed around the world. The response was the same as if Amelia Earhart had been found alive on a remote South Pacific island months after her disappearance in 1937 on her record-breaking flight around the world.

Reaction on Eye 1 was overwhelming, the crew ecstatic about the miraculous turn of events, their hard work and persistence onboard the most advanced submarine in the world rewarded with success.

The crew celebration lasted well into the night, with Hatch and Angela spending most of their time in Angela's cabin.

Congratulatory calls, e-mails, Facebook, and other social media posts about the rescue flooded Eye 1's communication links, with social media comments going viral around the world. Google News reported that Eye 1's great achievement in concert with French and United States Naval forces, received more hits than any other event since the Internet was invented. The public was going crazy.

Honeybunch called me saying, "Plug, I'm so proud of you, I can't wait till you get back home. Stay safe."

CHAPTER TWENTY-NINE
CALAMITY

The next day, everyone still groggy after the party the night before, I called a meeting of Eye 1's crew to decide what our next course of action would be.

I called on Angela for the latest report on Hurricane Rage which was barreling across the Atlantic Ocean with its sights set on the Caribbean islands.

"Hurricane Rage is gaining unprecedented strength, currently 600 miles southeast of Puerto Rico at Force 4, with the eye 115 miles in diameter and sustained winds already at 160 miles per hour," noted Angela, with her voice barely containing her excitement at this history-making meteorological event. "In order for us to intercept Hurricane Rage before it hits the Caribbean Islands we must leave right now for the United States base at Diego Garcia to catch our flight to Puerto Rico."

"Sean, how soon can we be at Diego Garcia?" I queried. "It is 2,200 miles from our present location."

"At full speed, we can be at Diego Garcia in seventeen hours," Sean responded.

I turned to Hatch and said, "Make way at all haste for Diego Garcia."

A C5A transport on standby at Diego Garcia was ready to load Eye 1 up and fly us to Puerto Rico so we could immediately head out to sea to enter the eye of Hurricane Rage. Once in the eye of the massive hurricane we would start taking readings to determine the exact path and intensity of Rage before it made landfall.

Arriving at Diego Garcia later the next day, Eye 1 was quickly loaded up on the C5A and we took off for San Juan, Puerto Rico.

Winds generated by Hurricane Rage were already being felt in San Juan, which was hunkering down to prepare for the massive storm. Windows were covered over with plywood, sandbags stockpiled, and residents in low-lying neighborhoods were evacuating to higher ground. Stores were flooded with people replenishing supplies in their disaster emergency kits including, food, water, flashlights, batteries, cash, and other essential items.

Onboard Eye 1, now docked in San Juan Naval Harbor, the crew made frenzied preparations prior to heading out to sea directly into the teeth of Hurricane

Rage. There was no turning back now, the entire Eye 1 organization geared up and ready for this baptism in fire, the first real test to see if Eye 1 would live up to its billing as a cutting-edge research boat. Could Eye 1 collect real-time hurricane data to protect lives and property, or was it another overpriced boondoggle?

The 95-mile diameter eye of Hurricane Rage was now 450 miles east of Puerto Rico, churning toward land with unprecedented force and fury, gaining strength as it drew energy from warmer waters near the coast.

Residents of Caribbean islands in the path of Rage were bracing for the superstorm by boarding up windows, stocking up on necessary supplies, moving to higher ground or into storm shelters. Panic had not set in, people following storm safety procedures drilled into them by regular hurricane events.

Eye 1 was rapidly moving to meet Hurricane Rage at its top speed of 127 mph, cruising at a depth of 1,000 feet, to avoid most underwater turbulence created by the massive storm.

The upper levels of the ocean are typically strongly stratified by temperature and salinity, colder, saltier water lying below warmer, fresher water near the surface. A hurricane mixes water up, resulting in cooler and saltier surface water and warmer and less salty deep water.

The colder surface water brought up from below is

a significant factor in controlling hurricane intensity. A strong, slow-moving hurricane will upwell cold water more effectively than a weaker and/or fast-moving hurricane. And since hurricanes require warm ocean water to fuel their engine, upwelling can weaken the storm. The trail of upwelled cooler water left behind a storm is called a cold wake, showing up clearly on maps of sea surface temperature.

Intense hurricanes can generate 60 foot plus waves, and at the ocean surface, the boundary between water and air becomes blurred. Amidst the formidable waves, sea spray and foam streak horizontally across the surface at high speed, whereas below the ocean's surface, currents and turbulence can also be very destructive.

Unlike places above the surface, the subsurface ocean doesn't go back to its normal state very quickly after a hurricane. Strong currents and turbulence exist up to a week after a storm. Damaging currents can extend down to at least 300 feet below the surface, capable of dismantling coral reefs, relocating shipwrecks, breaking oil pipelines, and displacing huge volumes of sand on the seabed.

In the Eye 1 command center I received a call from the White House, the president's voice causing me to jump two feet off the floor.

"Plug, on behalf of a grateful nation, I want to thank you, your crew, and the entire Eye 1 organization for finding MH370," President Tripp said. "Your successful effort locating MH370 not only put the historic plane disappearance mystery to rest, providing closure for families of the lost MH370 passengers and crew, but also freed Mr. X before the North Koreans broke him, preventing key quantum computing information from going to the North Koreans."

"Thank you, Mr. President," I responded. "We were happy to do it."

"Good luck with Hurricane Rage," the president continued. "It looks like this storm could put a lot of lives at risk."

Chapter Thirty
Into the Maelstrom

Heading toward Hurricane Rage 700 miles east in the North Atlantic at a depth of 1,500 feet, Hatch cranked Up Eye 1's speed to 127 mph, expecting to hit Rage's ever-expanding eyewall in under four hours. Current status of Rage was a Category 5 Hurricane with sustained winds of 195 mph and an eye diameter of seventy-five miles.

Storm models, including Angela's supercomputer readouts onboard Eye 1, were projecting that Hurricane Rage, moving west at about 10 mph, would hit Puerto Rico in thirty-nine hours, then strike the Dominican Republic before veering northwest toward Georgia. It was predicted that Rage would strike a glancing blow on the coastlines of South Carolina and North Carolina, then turn sharply northeast into the open Atlantic where it would fizzle out as a tropical storm.

To start taking more precise readings on Rage,

Hatch moved Eye 1 close to the surface so that it could extend aerials and sensors to collect precise real time data on the hurricane.

Excitement aboard Eye 1 was high, with the crew eagerly anticipating moving into the teeth of the storm at full action stations. Angela was in her glory gathering and analyzing storm data she relayed to shore stations with Eye 1's own powerful supercomputers dissecting Hurricane Rage information.

Hack was tweaking the storm analysis software code to optimize data gathering on Rage, developing quickly into a record-breaking monster superstorm.

On land, Puerto Rico was already feeling the effects of Hurricane Rage, with winds picking up to 85 mph and a storm surge already inundating coastal areas, citizens fleeing to higher ground with their belongings.

Storm warnings were put out on the United States mainland and observers were pleased that Hurricane Rage was projected to skirt Florida then make a glancing blow at the Carolinas before heading out into the North Atlantic Ocean.

The Eye 1 reality show TV crew aboard Eye 1 had their hands full monitoring cameras located inside and outside the sub and keeping tabs on frenzied crew activities as we prepared to head into the brunt of the storm.

"Great stuff folks, this is action central on steroids," Eye 1 TV crew boss Jeff Huston said.

Hatch was in his element in the captain's chair, steering the sub while exhorting crewmembers to be on their toes.

"Listen up, people," Hatch said. "This is where we make it or break it, there is no turning back now. Say your prayers and buckle up for the ride."

Eye 1 suddenly starting shaking due to extreme surface turbulence, and Hatch was forced to dive quickly to 250 feet while withdrawing surface antennas and sensors.

The ride smoothed out but Sean started yelling in the engine room, assessing possible damage caused by rough surface waters.

"Bloody hell," Sean shouted. "What are you people doing so close to the surface? We can't handle those types of stresses or we will break."

Hack's fingers were dancing all over the computer keyboard, optimizing performance of the weather data collection software and keeping the boat's navigational system working properly, a virtual Liberace in cyberspace.

"Goddang it guys," Hack enjoined. "This is the most fun I've had since I unraveled the Obamacare rollout disaster."

Doc Ozz was busy monitoring crewmembers' vital signs, worried that extreme stress might send someone over the edge, breaking a link in the chain that could send Eye 1 tumbling to the bottom of the ocean.

Ozz's main concern was me, after my psychogenic blackout on the trial cruise which set alarm bells off in the medical department.

"Plug, how are you doing?" Ozz asked me, my vital signs in the normal range.

"As good as can be expected, Doc," I said, "given that I'm hurtling into a Hurricane that is off the charts in terms of power and intensity. Let's put it this way, I haven't crapped my drawers yet."

Eye 1 nearing the eyewall of Hurricane Rage, Angela reported that major damage was occurring in Puerto Rico, with 2,700 people dead and 4,500 people missing. Hurricane Rage had leveled most structures and the storm surge had moved several miles inland, causing extensive flooding and drowning people as it went.

Puerto Ricans who had obeyed the hurricane warnings were hunkered down in shelters on higher ground, awaiting Hurricane Rage to die down and move further west toward the Dominican Republic and Haiti before they came out and surveyed the damage.

Hurricane Rage sustained winds were now 205 mph and steadily increasing, with an eye sixty miles wide and a barometric pressure now at 907 millibars, one of the lowest on record. All trees were leveled and bark torn off them by the catastrophic winds, likening this event to the Great Hurricane of 1780 which slammed Barbados with similar force, intensity, and resultant casualties. Hurricane Rage continued as a Force 5 Hurricane, edging its way off the charts toward Force 6, a classification that didn't exist, but was now needed to describe this cataclysmic weather event.

A flurry of activity was occurring at the National Hurricane Center in Florida, with staff in full emergency mode, issuing warnings and scrambling to predict the future path of Hurricane Rage as it neared the United States mainland. Fortunately, early models predicting that Rage would turn north after striking the Dominican Republic and Haiti, were holding firm as data streamed into the National Hurricane Center from Eye 1 and other conventional data-gathering sources.

Eye 1 was communicating with land stations via an exciting new underwater communications technology that involved Hurricane Hunter aircraft dropping untethered buoys along the route of Eye 1, enabling 24/7 voice and data communication from land to the research sub. The buoys were powered for three days, then automatically scuttled themselves to prevent adversaries from getting their hands on this cutting-edge technology.

With this new sub-communications system, Rane McCloud, head of the National Weather Service, was in constant contact with me and Angela aboard Eye 1, with Angela live-streaming meteorological data to the National Hurricane Center and other land stations.

"Plug, you are doing a great job out there," Rane said. "When you go through the Hurricane Rage eyewall, please be as close to the surface as you can to get the best readings possible. We need every scrap of data we can get."

"Will do," I replied.

CHAPTER THIRTY-ONE
TURBULENCE

As Eye 1 gradually surfaced near the Hurricane Rage eyewall, the crew was on edge, not sure of what to expect when we encountered the record-breaking force and fury of this colossal storm.

Rage sustained wind speeds were now 235 mph and heavy rains and towering thunderstorms marked the ring around the relatively calm eye of the hurricane. Waves now in excess of 100 feet high loomed over the tiny sub as it tried to find a safe place near the surface to extend its aerials and sensors.

Eye 1 was taking a severe pounding from all sides as Hatch guided it through the obstacle course of foaming waters jostling the sub as if it were in a washing machine.

"I don't know if we can take much more of this," Hatch yelled. "Get to emergency stations in case the hull fails. Anything can happen in these conditions."

The crew quickly readied the emergency gear

and prepared for the possibility of abandoning ship and subjecting themselves to the tempest outside. They knew their likelihood of survival in these furious waters was next to nothing.

I was almost blacking out as my seat restraints broke and I was thrown against a wall in the command center. Other crewmembers looked on in horror as I bounced off the wall and careened headfirst into the floor. I grabbed the base of my chair and held on for dear life, as the storm rolled over us and shook us violently, giving no quarter as we pushed forward toward the calm waters of Rage's eye.

The next thing we knew was getting caught in a massive whirlpool that turned us end over end as we submerged deeper and deeper into the frothing ocean.

Hack sent out a Mayday signal, as we prepared for the end.

Hatch, marshaling all his energy and concentration, held on to the joystick for dear life, trying to regain control of Eye 1 and save us from certain disaster. It didn't seem that our precious vessel could wrestle control back from the strengthening whirlpool.

In the engine room, Sean was doing everything he could to keep the nuclear reactor performing in these unimaginable conditions.

"Sean," Hatch shouted into his intercom, "I need

everything you have and then some."

Sean increased the power output of the reactor beyond specs and into the danger zone of an imminent meltdown. He then channeled the increased engine output to our lateral thrusters, attempting to push us away from certain doom in the clutches of the all-consuming vortex.

For a moment it looked like we weren't going to make it, our efforts not sufficient to break the grip of the unrelenting whirlpool.

Then, suddenly, the shaking stopped as Eye 1 passed into the calmer waters of Rage's eye, released from the powerful bonds of the eyewall.

Everyone let out a great sigh of relief, undoing their seat belts and hugging their colleagues with unbridled joy. For my part, I was in shock, trying to get my bearings back after being viciously tossed around in the command center.

Our next task was moving into the center of the storm to get detailed readings on the current status of Hurricane Rage, which was evolving into the nightmare storm of the ages. It amazed me how calm conditions were in the eye, when moments before we were being pummeled mercilessly from all corners. The blue skies above gave us the false sense that all was well, that things might be okay again.

Back in Puerto Rico, record wind, rains, and flooding were lashing the territory with unrelenting fury, portending far worse things to come when the full force of Hurricane Rage was expected to hit Puerto Rico in about fourteen hours. Puerto Ricans were fleeing to higher ground in the millions, trying to find safe refuge from the apocalyptic catastrophe. Tens of thousands of homes were already destroyed and thousands of lives had been snuffed out as Rage intensified.

Nearing the center of Hurricane Rage's eye, Eye 1 slowed down in the deceptively calm waters around it, cruising on the surface with all weather data-gathering systems deployed and fully engaged. Angela was in her element, analyzing storm data as it streamed into the supercomputers, trying to make sense of the storm as it built toward its crescendo.

"I am getting some new results here indicating that Rage could be shifting from its original course toward the Carolinas," Angela expostulated. "Our current weather models may be totally wrong."

Conferring on the phone with Rane McCloud at the National Hurricane Center, Angela explained her new theory and McCloud was confounded by the news.

"Is there any way you can confirm the implications of this new data set before we raise alarm bells and broadcast the course correction to the public?" Rane asked Angela. "We must be sure about this, there is too much at stake here."

"Well, there is one way we can do that, but it is very risky," Angela responded. "Hack has come up with a new portable device with all our sensor apparatus built into it. I could go topside and give it a try."

"Please do," Rane continued. "We have no other option."

An Eye 1 crew meeting quickly ensued, with me and Hatch leading the chorus to not allow Angela up on the sub's observation deck. With unpredictable conditions outside, anything could happen to her, and it just wasn't worth it.

Angela strongly rebuffed these sentiments, saying, "We must be completely sure about our new projections. Cross-checking this data with the portable sensor unit is absolutely necessary."

With millions of lives on the line, Hatch and I reluctantly agreed with Angela's request, asserting that all safety measures must be taken while Angela was out there taking her readings.

Angela quickly donned her survival suit and climbed up the ladder to the small topside observation deck. Attaching her tether to the railing, she prepared to activate the sophisticated weather sensor array attached to her body by a strong strap positioned under her armpit and around her neck.

Conditions outside seemed benign at the moment, with light winds and calm seas providing a false sense of security for the courageous meteorologist.

Angela finished taking her readings and prepared to go below. Unhooking the tether, Angela turned around to open the hatch when all hell broke loose. A freak wave, about thirty feet high, swept Angela off the sub into the ocean, causing her to struggle violently in the now churned-up seas, drifting away from the sub at an alarming speed.

In the command center everyone immediately went into emergency mode, trying to put their panic aside while working to rescue Angela from her life-threatening ordeal.

Beside himself with anxiety about the fate of his cherished girlfriend and soul mate, Hatch commanded the room with his intensity.

"Doc and I must go out there in our exoskeletons to bring her back," Hatch exhorted. "There is no other choice."

The rest of the crew quickly assented to Hatch's request, knowing there was no other option to save their indispensable crewmate.

Ten minutes later Hatch and Doc were in the water, speeding toward Angela through turbulent seas in their dolphin speed suits.

Fortunately, a high-precision GPS tracker was attached to Angela's survival suit, enabling Hatch and Doc to track her location on their Hack-designed dive watches.

Angela was now 1,400 yards away from Eye 1, the fast current steering her toward the eastern eyewall of Hurricane Rage moving westward at an alarming speed, threatening to ensnare the swimmers in a death cauldron.

Hatch and Doc steadily gained on Angela, reaching her just as seas picked up and she was being jostled around in every direction. Grabbing Angela on either side, Hatch and Doc started pulling her back toward Eye 1, steadily narrowing the gap between Angela and safety.

Back onboard the sub, Hatch and Angela embraced and kissed, knowing she had narrowly escaped a violent end.

Regaining her composure, Angela got back to business and connected the portable sensor unit to the supercomputers, enabling the new data to interface with existing Hurricane Rage weather models to provide an updated projection regarding the savage hurricane's path, speed, and intensity.

Her eyes widening as she examined the revised weather models on her computer screen, Angela exclaimed, "Hurricane Rage is now heading directly toward Miami with landfall in approximately 24 hours. This will be a total disaster. Rage will be off the scale at Force 7, with 300+ mph sustained winds, 38 inches of rain, and a storm surge of 55 feet. Most of southern Florida will be underwater."

CHAPTER THIRTY-TWO
VINDICATION

The Eye 1 crew reacted in disbelief, knowing the devastating damage that would follow when Hurricane Rage hit Miami and the rest of southern Florida.

Plug immediately placed a conference call with National Weather Service Chief Rane McCloud, Florida's Governor E.Z. Living, and President Tripp at the White House.

"We will not have time to evacuate everyone," Florida Governor E.Z. Living said. "The freeways will be jammed with traffic. Most citizens will have to shelter in place."

The President concurred with this assessment, saying, "A Berlin type airlift will be conducted to get as many people out as we can. I have already given orders to get the airlift rolling. All US government air assets, including Defense Department aircraft, will be in the air right away. Plus, the civilian air fleet has been asked to participate in this operation.

"But that won't be enough, millions will die," Governor Living interjected. "What else can we do?"

I cut into the conversation, saying, "As many people as possible who can't get out will be loaded on giant inflatable rafts that have been pre-positioned throughout Florida. Raft passengers will ride out the storm until floodwaters recede."

Funded by the Eye 1 foundation, these mega-sized rafts held 500 people each and were located in storage sheds near open areas around Florida. The rafts could be quickly inflated and loaded with nearby residents who are contacted via phone, TV, radio, e-mail, text, social media, and emergency loudspeakers. Emergency personnel in each area would conduct loading of the rafts.

The Eye 1 Foundation rafts were specially designed with hundreds of self-sealing air chambers reducing the effect of punctures in the craft. The self-repairing chambers used the same technology as run-flat car tires. Food, supplies, and water for several weeks were stored on the rafts. The rafts would be filled on a first-come, first-served basis with children, parents, the elderly, and first responders having boarding priority, so that emergency personnel could quickly go to work helping, feeding, and treating people soon after floodwaters subsided.

The rafts were tethered to concrete stanchions

embedded in the ground that utilized automatic winches to play out or reel in the Kevlar cables as the water level went up and down. Special body belts for each passenger would secure them to the raft, preventing people from getting blown out by the rampaging winds. The weight of the raft with all the people and supplies in it would prevent the craft from getting blown away.

Eye 1's role in the ongoing conflagration was to provide continuous, real-time data from the heart of Hurricane Rage as the epic superstorm proceeded toward southern Florida.

Scurrying back and forth in the command center carrying out their vital work, Eye 1 crewmembers each quietly acknowledged the affirmation of their project. Precious hours had been gained for Floridians by Eye 1, enabling these citizens to better prepare for the worst storm in recorded history. Millions of lives would be saved by the little sub that could.

For my part, the wishful thinking of a dreamer was now real.

Dream on.

Stay tuned...

About the Author

Raised in Salmon Arm, British Columbia, Canada, Dean Landers started reading at the age of five and has never stopped. His earliest published writing experience was 'Trails to the Shuswap', the first outdoor recreation guidebook of the Shuswap Lake area. After college, Dean worked as a newspaper reporter followed by serving as a wilderness recreation mapper and firefighter for the British Columbia Forest Service.

In 1984 Dean came to the United States to get married and conceived and published the 'Great Outdoors USA' outdoor recreation map series. He then ran a small property management business for many years before semi-retiring in 2016 to write books and work on his Go Soak It! Fire Buster System invention, a newly patented product available on Amazon.com that protects homes from wildfires. Dean enjoys his family, swimming, golf and a good conversation when he can get it.

65468966R00129

Made in the USA
Lexington, KY
13 July 2017